The Council of Animals

The Council
of Animals

Nick McDonell

With illustrations by
Steven Tabbutt

Henry Holt and Company **H** New York

Henry Holt and Company
Publishers since 1866
120 Broadway
New York, New York 10271
www.henryholt.com

Henry Holt® and Ⓗ® are registered trademarks of
Macmillan Publishing Group, LLC.

Library of Congress Cataloging-in-Publication Data

Names: McDonell, Nick, 1984- author. | Tabbutt, Steven, illustrator.
Title: The council of animals / Nick McDonell ; with illustrations by
    Steven Tabbutt.
Description: First edition. | New York : Henry Holt and Company, 2021.
Identifiers: LCCN 2020034390 (print) | LCCN 2020034391 (ebook)
    | ISBN 9781250799036 (hardcover) | ISBN 9781250799043
    (ebook)
Subjects: LCSH: Human-animal relationships—Fiction. | GSAFD:
    Dystopias.
Classification: LCC PS3613.C388 C68 2021 (print) | LCC PS3613.C388
    (ebook) | DDC 813/.6—dc23
LC record available at https://lccn.loc.gov/2020034390
LC ebook record available at https://lccn.loc.gov/2020034391

Our books may be purchased in bulk for promotional, educational,
or business use. Please contact your local bookseller or the Macmillan
Corporate and Premium Sales Department at (800) 221-7945,
extension 5442, or by e-mail at
MacmillanSpecialMarkets@macmillan.com.

First Edition 2021

Designed by Meryl Sussman Levavi

Creative direction of illustration by Christopher Sergio

Printed in the United States of America

1 3 5 7 9 10 8 6 4 2

To

Orla

Trym

Allen

Eliott

Cerys

Felix

Edgar

Ayla

and

P.J.

The Council
of Animals

Chapter 1

The animals decided to vote. They chose a location more convenient to some than others.

It was a vast superyacht, grounded upon a cliff, high above the sea. A bulldog arrived first. He was grizzled, mostly grey, and arthritic. His undershot jaw, however, retained much of its fierce, stubborn strength. He was a determined-looking sort of dog. Limping into the shade of a smashed helicopter—fallen from its place on the yacht's deck—he sniffed the wind for creatures. He smelled none and so lay down, snout upon paws, to wait. Anticipating the difficulty of the journey, he had left his pack before dawn and was, in fact, early.

Next came a horse, trotting—idiotically, thought the dog—in zigzags, toward the yacht. His almond coat was glossy and his mane was streaked blond from sunshine. A brilliant white stripe ran down his muzzle. He slowed to a panting rest. Catching his breath, he nosed for something to eat in the weeds beside the dog.

"Good afternoon," said the dog.

"Where are the sugar cubes?"

"Sugar cubes?"

"Sometimes they have sugar cubes."

"None of *them* are here."

The horse appeared to think about this.

"That's the point," added the dog.

"Carrots?"

Dog and horse regarded each other for a long moment.

"No carrots either."

. . . *You bloody fool*, added the dog, internally.

The horse continued nosing in the weeds. "The cat told me to tell you she'll be late," he said, through a mouthful of dandelions.

Before the dog had time to complain about this, the horse snapped his head up in alarm and looked down the promontory. Though it had been agreed no animal should harm another for the duration of the meeting, he could not banish instinct. He smelled the bear before he saw her.

The dog, too. Together they watched her pad along, ropey muscles rolling beneath her fur.

"I thought it would be a snow bear," whispered the horse.

"Polar bear," corrected the dog.

This bear was a grizzly, and though certainly fearsome from afar she was not, really, a very strong or well-fed bear. She looked rather scruffy, in fact. Harried.

"Good afternoon," said the dog, as the bear joined them in the shade.

"Have the others arrived?" asked the bear.

"Not yet," said the dog.

"The cat told me to tell you she'll be late," repeated the horse.

"No surprises there, eh?" said the dog, hoping to befriend the bear.

But the bear only grunted. Perhaps it would be a long wait. She pawed her way into the broken helicopter's cockpit. Rummaging about, she was pleased to discover a spiral-bound flight manual. She hooked it with a claw and carried it out to the grass.

The bear looked at helicopter diagrams, the horse ate, and soon the dog dozed off.

He hadn't been asleep long when a striped cat arrived. Purring, she rubbed along the horse's great hooves, then nodded respectfully at the bear and found herself a perch in the crashed helicopter, upon one of its soft, upholstered seats.

The cat had just begun grooming a leg when, with a

sharp *caaw!*, a crow announced himself. He descended in spirals and landed on one of the propeller blades.

"Bird blessings on you," said the crow, by way of greeting.

And then, almost as soon as the crow had landed, the ringing of a bell cut the seaside air.

As one, the animals looked up to the source of the sound. It was a yellow-eyed baboon, peering at them from a hatch in the yacht's deck, high above. In one pink hand this baboon held a brass bell, which he shook again with great vigor before stowing it in a small bag he wore over his shoulder.

"Order!" shouted the baboon. "We'll begin! For victory!"

The bear closed the flight manual and the horse stopped chewing dandelions. This baboon seemed very excited. He clambered down the deck and landed neatly beside the dog.

"I'm up, I'm up," insisted the dog, though he'd been fast asleep.

"But, baboon," said the bear, "we can't begin. We're not all here."

"Yes, the cats are late as usual," added the dog. "Very disrespectful."

"This dog must still be sleeping," said the cat in the cockpit, and the horse whinnied with laughter.

A look of great frustration darkened the dog's square face. "I was just . . . thinking!"

"*We* are all here—" said the baboon.

"Bird blessings," interrupted the crow, "on all creatures!"

"Bird Gods are important! Very important," agreed the baboon, before turning to the bear. "All of *us* are here. Anyone who is not here is not *us*. That's *we*. So *we* can begin."

"But if the others aren't here," said the bear, slowly, focusing on one bit of the problem, "how will they decide how to vote?"

"They vote as we tell them," said the baboon. "Animals like that."

The bear frowned. "Still," she said, "I think it is better not to rush."

"Horse," said the baboon, ignoring the bear, "I looked everywhere, I worked very hard—very hard!—and found this for you."

And the baboon produced from his shoulder bag a yellow box. He ripped off its top with his teeth and set it down for the horse.

The box, the animals saw, was full of brown sugar.

In a blink, the horse snuffled it all up. He even began chewing on the box.

"Where did you get that?" asked the dog.

"Only I can get it for you," said the baboon. "Only I!"

"I could get it, too," said the crow. "Praise be to The Egg."

"Dog," said the bear, who did not want to be distracted

from the issue at paw, "don't you agree: better not to rush our vote?"

The dog, puffing out his chest, was pleased to be consulted. He decided he would say something wise about how, in the wars, it was always better not to rush.

But before he had managed to say anything, the baboon was talking again.

"Not rush?" exclaimed the baboon. "But we *have*

to rush! For *safety*! For our *victory*, right, dog? We must have *order*!"

The dog, now confused, hesitated.

"I disagree," purred the cat.

"Fully agreed!" said the dog. He disagreed with cats, on printsiple.

(Though which printsiple it was, he could not precisely say.)

"That settles it," said the baboon. "Crow! Call us to order!"

"But," said the bear, "but—"

The crow cawed out, in his powerful voice:

"Animal council in ORDER!"

The dog saluted. The cat sighed and shook her head.

"All animals," the crow continued, "make their mark!"

In their respective ways, each animal marked territory. The bear scratched her back against the yacht; the dog peed on it. The cat rubbed her cheeks against the helicopter seat; the horse dropped a dung pile. The baboon howled and slapped the ground. The crow sang out his song, then pronounced:

"*Caw!* The question is set, with the blessing of the Bird Gods, by previous animal council! The Animal Kingdoms listen and agree, in the light of The Egg! *Caw . . .*"

"Takes a minute to get going, doesn't he?" muttered the dog to the bear.

"And with nest blessings we pray for wisdom in our vote. WHEREBY: The Calamity destroyed the ecosystems of many eggs and animals! WHEREBY: humans caused The Calamity!"

Here the baboon hissed and bared his teeth. The crow continued.

". . . and WHEREBY: only a few humans survived The Calamity! RESOLVED: the Animal Kingdom, represented by the ambassadors here marking their territory, shall, to protect against further Calamity . . . *Eat all the humans!* Animals, how do you vote: *YAY OR NAY?!*"

"I can't believe it has come to this," whispered the bear to the cat.

"It's not over," whispered back the cat.

"*Caw!*" called the crow. "It has been agreed by rabbit procedure that the DOG shall speak and cast his vote first. I yield to the dog. *Caw!*"

Chapter 2

$\mathcal{S}$ome background.

Animals have, of course, always communicated. Many work together to mutual advantage—like oxpeckers and rhinoceroses, for example, who both benefit when oxpeckers eat ticks out of a rhino's hide. Or hyenas and buzzards, whose mutual understanding of quantum mechanics has been much enriched by their full moon gatherings. While some animals prefer solitude—pigeons are obviously more social than snow leopards—no animal lives in total isolation. Communication—interspecies and intraspecies—is constant. Even bony zompompers at the bottom of the Marianas Trench like to chat with blue whales now and then.

Humans, however, never communicated with animals. Let alone attended their formal meetings. This was not for want of invitation from the animals. Often enough, any animal would tell you, they'd *tried* to communicate with humans. But humans spoke only their own human languages. They did not speak *grak*.

There was much division of opinion as to why this should be. Grak, the animal *lingua franca*, was spoken by every other species. All were bilingual. Some animals said that humans were simply too stupid to speak grak. Others, that humans were physiologically incapable. Other animals insisted that humans *had* spoken grak in the past but had forgotten how. Still others believed that *some* humans had spoken grak—and some still might— but *stronger* humans forbade the language as part of a plot to rule all the other creatures. Those exceptional humans who did speak grak, several ancient and highly regarded tortoises argued, tended to be environmentalists, artists, mystics—humans often persecuted by their fellows.

Such persecution, the tortoises observed, had crescendoed in the years before The Calamity.

All suffered in The Calamity. But when the toxic fog cleared, humans—populationwise, proportionally—had suffered most. The last of them, perhaps a dozen, were living in a small camp, not so far from where the council was being held.

As we heard the crow announce, the council concerned these remaining humans. Certain animals had suggested that, since humans were responsible for The Calamity, and so might multiply and cause *another* Calamity, it would be wise to kill and eat them. All of them. Eat all the humans.

There would, no doubt, be animal casualties. But in a showdown between the few remaining humans and all the animals on earth, the animals would win. And then the planet would be safe. Thus the council and vote.

Each of the animals at the council was a species ambassador, chosen (some more democratically than others) by their fellows. It had been agreed that each would have an opportunity to speak before voting.

The order of speakers had been agreed at the previous meeting, after a venerable rabbit had been devoured over questions of procedure.

Chapter 3

"Now I am an old dog, but I know men."

The dog had been thinking about how to begin his speech for several days.

"I have seen the best and worst of men. War brings both."

The cat rolled her eyes.

"Before The Calamity, I traveled with a human general. The men were at war, which is the best thing men do, because war requires constant training. Training! There's nothing better. Imagine a thousand sticks, thrown over and over. Imagine a *million* sticks. Imagine searching for hidden smells, and when you find them—rewards! That's war. *Plus* pointing at prey. Not just rabbits or squirrels—but other men! Men who, we knew for a fact, *forbade bacon*! For these were the bacon wars. Who among us has had bacon?"

"Bacon," agreed the bear, "is excellent."

"I have seen men—"

"Domesticated!" the baboon howled, interrupting. "*That's* why you like bacon. Smoked pig meat! Not for wild animals. Lazy, lazy, terrible."

"*I'm* a wild animal," growled the bear, sitting up on her haunches.

Surprised by the bear's anger, the baboon bared his teeth and rang his bell, and so the cat hissed and arched her back, and the horse whinnied and stamped his feet, and the crow cawed, and the dog barked angrily.

But presently all the animals recovered their composure.

"Where was I?" asked the dog, embarrassed he'd lost his train of thought.

"You've seen men at war," said the bear.

"Yes, outstanding—I slept in the general's quarters, but I met daily with my dogs. Finer creatures I've never known. We faced terrible threats. Why and how was classified. All my mutts and I knew was that"—the dog sniffed, on the verge of tears, and pawed at his eyes—"we were at . . . war. Fur everywhere. Bloody whiskers. Tails on fire."

The dog collected himself.

"The men gave treats to those hero dogs. *Treats*. Please, a moment of silence for the dogs who died."

The dog stood at attention and saluted.

"This dog doesn't know what the war was about," the bear whispered to the cat, in the silent moment.

The cat only sighed.

"And now," resumed the dog, "we are to turn on men, in their darkest hour? Kill and eat them? No, I say. We must fight by their side, as we have since they captured fire. We're not their servants—we'll still eat their corpses— but we *are* their allies. We dogs have led humans to the moon, and they cared for us. And now, after The Calamity, if we are to sit again, we know what we sit for. We sit for honor! And freedom! And demoscratchy!"

And then the dog, as though commanding himself, shouted: "Sit!"

And he sat. And then:

"Down!"

And he lay down. And: "Roll over!"

And the dog rolled himself over, tongue lolling out.

"Very bizarre behavior," whispered the bear to the cat. "He's repeating human slogans."

"Shake," shouted the dog, and held out a paw toward the baboon.

But the baboon only spat a great wad of phlegm down into the dandelions.

"You see," said the dog, "we are our own masters."

And then the baboon, picking up a stick, looked into the dog's rheumy eyes.

"Fetch," said the baboon, hurling the stick.

The dog, old as he was, ran off after it.

The baboon turned to the bear, snarling: "You would vote with this fool?"

"He is, perhaps, confused—" conceded the bear.

"Demoscratchy?" the cat commented, yawning.

"You are not wild," said the baboon. "Your domestication caused The Calamity!"

"Sugar cubes!" interrupted the horse, stamping his hooves.

The other animals, falling silent, looked at him.

"More sugar cubes?"

"I can get some, soon," cooed the baboon.

The horse continued eating dandelions, and the dog returned, panting.

"Mission accomplished!" said the dog, dropping the stick.

✦

This chronicle concerns all the animals of earth but focuses on a handful, at a key moment, a precipice. Their . . . ordinariness must be evident already, to the sensitive reader.

That *these* are the animals—subsequently so famous, even legendary—who cast the fateful vote, played such crucial roles in the momentous events which followed, may come as a surprise, even a disappointment. Perhaps we imagine history's great moments turn on the backs of more dignified creatures. Perhaps even heroes.

But what is a hero? Were the Pharaonic cats as wise as myth suggests? Or were they simply shrewd rat catchers? And were the first rats to circumnavigate the globe as bold as Magellan? Or were they simply hungry stowaways?

Desire,
as the walruses say,
is better insulation
than virtue. This is true for heroes
as well as any ordinary animal. Of
course, it is not the business of the
narrator (whose identity will be
made known in due course) to
make such pronouncements. It
is rather to report what actually happened and let the
reader draw their own conclu-
sions.

Chapter 4

"Now the horse speaks! The dog is finished! Now the horse!"

The baboon hopped from one foot to the other.

"Now wait, please," said the bear, slowly as usual. "We should mark the vote. That way, when everyone arrives they can see how we voted."

"I will tell them," said the baboon.

This was not good enough for the bear, who began to carve the tally into a nearby tree with one of her claws.

"What are you doing?" demanded the baboon.

"Keeping track," said the bear. "There, have a look."

This is what the bear had carved:

"Outstanding," said the dog.

"Fine," said the baboon. "One vote for humans. Now the horse!"

Sensing he was being watched, the horse took his nose out of the weeds.

"Horse," said the bear, "what do the horses want for the humans? Live or die?"

The horse hesitated, then lifted his head up high and said: "We want bananas."

A moment of confused silence.

The horse, with growing anxiety, looked to the baboon.

"You said I should say I want bana—"

"Point of order!" shouted the baboon. "Now is the time for points of order!"

"Wait a moment," said the bear. "Baboon, are you

telling the horse what to say? The horses must speak for themselves."

"And what if I am?"

"This is about more than sugar and bananas," said the bear. "The decision we make—"

"Is important, very, very important! Which is why it must be *right*, which is why I am helping the horse!"

"But animals should decide for themselves, in their own interest. Horses don't need bananas—"

The cat dragged a claw over the metal of the helicopter, making a terrible screeching noise. The bear and baboon both clapped their paws over their ears.

"Let's get on with it," said the cat, "shall we?"

"But cat," cried the bear, feeling rather betrayed, "each animal must decide on their own. One animal, one vote!"

"And how," sighed the cat, rolling on her back and stretching, "is one animal to decide, except by listening to the other animals?"

"Hear the Bird Gods! Hear them! Praise to The Egg!"

"Praise to The Egg!" agreed the baboon.

"Horse," purred the cat, "please continue."

The horse stamped his hooves. "It is my time to speak."

"Yes it is."

"I am a horse. I will speak!"

"Please proceed, horse."

"Since I was a foal, I liked to run," said the horse. "I liked the *du dum du dum du dum. . . .*"

He shook his great head.

"When the day of my first race came, I was proud! I never threw my jockey. I loved him. I was a good horse. After my races I would live in a green pasture and eat clover with my mother. *We have to win the race! We have to win the race!* The crowd cheered. I won. Then I was taken away. They put me in . . . an airplane."

"No!" shouted the bear.

"Yes," the horse said, "an airplane."

"Aaaoooooo!" howled the dog.

The baboon spat another wad of phlegm, and the cat shook her head sadly.

"The sky is for birds!" cawed the crow, summing up the animals' feeling on the matter.

"I saw day and night out the window," said the horse, continuing his story. "There was no green pasture and clover, no mother. I was taken to a new barn, with new riders, a new human language. I was in polo."

"What is polo?" asked the bear.

"See!" said the baboon. "The bear is ignorant! The bear does not know what polo is! The bear is stupid, stupid."

"A human mating dance," said the horse. "They have sticks to hit a ball across a field. The man who hits the ball mates with the best woman. They wear white pants and no spurs."

"I think," said the cat, quietly, "it's also a *game*. Horse, do you know where you played? The name of the place?"

"Argengolia. I was a champion. Their sticks hit my knees, my jockey mated, I galloped. But then . . . they did not keep me. They put me back on . . ."

"No!" growled the bear.

". . . an airplane."

"Aaaaooooo!" howled the dog.

"The sky is for birds!" cawed the crow.

"Why did they fly me? I liked to race, but racing was not . . . good? I liked to polo, but polo was not . . . good? They flew me to another place, a ranch by the sea. Only one woman lived there. I ate and trotted around a ring. Some days I carried the woman through fields. She fed me carrots and sugar cubes."

Here, the horse's eyes clouded over. Great salty teardrops quivered on his long lashes.

The cat leapt down from her perch and nuzzled the horse's hooves comfortingly. Looking up, she saw the scars from the polo mallets up and down the horse's legs.

"She gave me sugar cubes," resumed the horse. "One day we rode in a field of peppers and we saw a man beat a donkey. We galloped over. The woman dismounted and yelled. Other men stopped picking peppers and watched. And then, the man who beat the donkey . . . *beat the woman.* The donkey told me: RUN! So I ran. The donkey was slow, but we ran together."

"What happened to the woman?" asked the bear.

"I don't know. I wanted to find her, but the donkey said no, and he took my bit and threw it in the sea."

"Victory!" said the baboon.

"The donkey told me, men in the field always beat donkeys," said the horse. "He told me humans are . . . greedy. We could *all* have the sugar and the oats—there is enough for everyone—but humans are like magpies."

The animals all waited for the horse to continue, but the horse said nothing.

"And?" prompted the dog.

"And . . . The Calamity happened," said the horse.

"And how do the horses vote?" asked the baboon, hopping foot to foot.

"We vote to kill the humans," said the horse, without hesitation.

"Great Scott, why?" cried the dog.

"You said you loved your jockey!" said the bear.

"The horse has cast his vote!" shouted the baboon. "Mark it!"

The bear looked to the cat, who shrugged, and to the crow, but he only nibbled lice out of his feathers.

And so the bear marked a vote against humanity.

"Point of order," said the baboon, grinning, "point of order, voting adjourned. Recess!"

"There's no point of order for recess!" said the bear.

But the baboon was already climbing up the yacht, eager to attend to secret business.

Chapter 5

Higher and higher the baboon climbed. He swung from stanchion to line, leapt along the railings of the superyacht. Toward the top, he popped through an open hatch.

Inside was gloomy and damp. Because the yacht was overturned, the baboon walked on walls rather than the floor. Arriving in the galley, he yanked open a pantry door. All manner of dry goods were scattered about, and the baboon crouched among the sacks and boxes and tins, rooting for his prize. Flour, no, beans, no, cooking oil, no, but finally . . . sugar!

The bag of sugar was too big for him to carry. With

his sharp teeth he gnawed wider the hole he'd made on a previous visit. Looking about, he found a yellow box of biscuits, which he tore open and shook out, stuffing several biscuits in his mouth. He would use the empty box to carry some more sugar to the horse.

The baboon was about to go, but the biscuits had made his mouth dry. He remembered a cooler of water down the hall which had somehow survived the capsizing of the superyacht. He would stop for a drink, to wash down the biscuits.

But then, climbing out of the galley, he heard a noise.

The echoing silence of the yacht was broken by . . . a scuttling . . . a scraping, scratching . . .

The baboon, peering around a corner, came snout to antennae with a cockroach.

"Aaah!" yelped the baboon.

(For even baboons are frightened of cockroaches.)

"Greetings, comrade," chirped the cockroach. "Welcome! Are you hungry? We have much to share."

"I was going to drink," said the baboon, edging toward the cooler.

"There is plenty of water," said the roach. "Turn the spigot."

The baboon fiddled with the spigot. The roach was making him nervous. He had never spoken with a roach. And the spigot was stuck. The baboon twisted and twisted but he could not open it up.

"Comrades," chirped the roach, "help our brother baboon."

From every dark cranny of the yacht, swarms of roaches emerged, scuttling to the water cooler.

The baboon was frozen, terrified.

And then the roaches began to sing. The melody fell somewhere between "Take Me Out to the Ball Game" and "Auld Lang Syne."

Insects of jungle and seashore
Insects of every clime
Turn your antennae to me now
And know the truth of our time!
Before crustaceans and cetaceans
Before all lizards and toads
We were the masters of this planet
And we're returning to glories of old!
Arise you roaches from your burrows
Arise all you lice and flies
Burrow into the skin of the mammals
Lay your eggs behind their eyes!
Because it's sting, and bite, and nest, my dears
Soon, we'll even the score
The warm bloods who wrecked our home will be gone
And insects will rule once more!
The Amazon will rise again
There'll be no pesticide

Concrete will crumble back to dust
And we'll never drink fluoride!
We've lived five hundred million years
We'll live five hundred still
The mammals' time has come and gone
It's time for bugs to kill!
Insects of jungle and seashore
Insects of every clime
Turn your antennae to me now
And know the truth of our time!

The baboon trembled. The roaches, like a black undulating carpet, carried the water cooler up to the ceiling and then dropped it down: *BANGCRRACKWHOOSH!*

Dozens of roaches were squashed, and more were swept away in the spilt water. But they didn't seem to mind.

"Thirsty?" said the roach who had first startled the baboon. "Drink!"

The baboon, quite certain the masses of roaches were going to attack, was paralyzed.

"Go on," said the roach, "drink and get back to your vote."

Seeing the baboon's surprise, the roach laughed its peculiar laugh—a high-pitched sound, a bit like the smashing of a tiny piano.

"How did you know?"

"You thought we didn't know about your vote?" said

the roach. "Of course we know! We always know! And we're never invited."

"But, but, it has always been like that," said the baboon. "You bugs never wanted to join the councils anyway!"

"Didn't we? Or were we just never asked? No matter. Humans, baboons. You're all mammals. You all share the blame. And the time is coming. . . ."

Just as quickly as they'd emerged, the cockroaches scuttled into the yacht walls.

"Wait!" cried the baboon. "Baboons have never been enemies of the insects! If you don't want to join the council, good! There *are* too many mammals! Let's make a deal! We can make a good, good deal!"

And the spokesroach twitched its antennae at the baboon, as if in thought.

Chapter 6

Meanwhile, back on the cliff, bear, cat, and dog stood beside a pile of sticks.

The crow perched on a branch above. The horse was off to the side, eating dandelions.

"Ready?" asked the bear.

The dog nodded, wagging his stumpy tail.

"Okay, crow," said the bear, "go ahead."

The crow turned his shining black eyes on the dog. Then he swooped down and, grabbing a stick from the pile, cawed out: "Fetch!"

Flapping upward, he flung the stick away.

The dog, without hesitation, took off running.

"No!" cried the bear in frustration. "Stop!"

But the dog was gone.

Soon he returned with the stick. Seeing the expression on the bear's face, he dropped it and looked at the ground.

"I've done it again, haven't I," he said, gloomily.

"It's okay," said the bear. "Now remember, this time, no matter what anyone says, *don't fetch.*"

The next time, as the dog took off running, the bear only sighed.

"Might as well give up," said the cat. "New trick."

"No!" insisted the bear. "We can teach him to be a free thinker."

"Bear, don't you see? You're just trading one form of training for another."

"I'm educating him."

"He's *been* educated. He went to the best of schools. Woof Point, I believe."

"That's not education, that's indoctrination."

The dog trotted back with a stick in his jaws.

"Even if he wasn't an old dog," said the cat, "no one *really* thinks for himself. Everyone fetches for someone."

"Well, who's your master, then?"

"Nature."

The bear threw her paws in the air. The dog dropped his stick, tail wagging. It took him several moments to decipher the bear's disappointed expression.

"Dammit!" said the dog.

The cat laughed. The bear, incensed, picked up another stick and waved it at the cat. The dog's eyes followed.

"Fine, cat. Laugh. But it's learning that sets us apart from rocks and trees. Why else would we be able to speak grak? Or hold animal councils? We *learned*. And in the learning and relearning, time and again, we make a better Animal Kingdom. It's just . . . *bad ideas* that cause problems, that make us fetch. By nature, individually, each of us, we're *good*!"

"Throw the stick!" said the dog. "Throw it, throw it!"

"Look," said the cat, "that paragon of virtue, the baboon, has returned."

The baboon, now among them again, rang his bell.

"Order, order! We resume the vote. Horse, here is some more sugar!"

"That's bribery!" said the bear. "And why should *you* get to decide the points of order? You left!"

"I didn't leave," said the baboon.

"We all saw you go!"

The baboon slapped his hands on the ground.

"I went to protect you! For safety!"

"To protect us from what?"

"There are bad animals making plans!"

"If we must fight," said the dog, "we fight."

"No one's fighting," said the bear.

"Bird Gods, shield us with your feathers!" cawed the crow.

"We don't need shielding," said the bear. "The baboon is making it all up!"

"Bear," said the cat, "remain calm. How will you vote? Tell us."

"But the bribery!"

"There's nothing to do about it, bear," said the cat. "You can't reverse a vote, everyone knows that. So let's get on with it."

"Fine," said the bear. And with a mighty sigh she began her speech.

"Hear me, animals: we must not kill and eat all the humans. We must help them. Not because of what they have done or what they are, but because of what they *can be*. The clever baboon tells you they were unnatural. The Calamity was unnatural. Maybe so. It is better to prevent another. Maybe so. But what is more unnatural than extinction? The baboon, no doubt, is clever. But like the dog, I was a friend to men. I was a bear in Hollywood, a movie bear. An actor."

The bear sat back up on her hind legs to continue her speech, gesturing broadly.

"The baboon says they were my masters, and the baboon is clever. But when my kind was waning, even going extinct, some men protected lands for us and forbade the hunting of our kind. They learned balance and attempted to maintain it. Were they our masters then? And when in ages lost men ranged with herds of caribou and bison and worshipped us, were they our masters

then? I did not know the master worshipped his sub-
ject. But the baboon says they were our masters, and the
baboon is clever. You know that men could have killed
and eaten us all many times over—but instead, some
men, when they crowded the earth, renounced meat.
Were those men our masters? But the baboon says they
would master us all, and the baboon is a clever animal. I
speak not to call the baboon foolish—we all know he is
not. I speak only what I know. Sometimes, all you animals have loved men. Even you, crow, perched upon the
shoulders of their scholars. And you, horse, you recall
the way they gave you sugar. If we resolve to kill them
all, we animals have lost the scent."

Here she stopped. "Bear with me a moment," said the
bear, "my heart is with the men, and I must pause, while
it returns."

"The bear speaks the truth," growled the dog, and
saluted.

The baboon spat another wad of phlegm into the
dandelions.

"Horse," said the bear, "no sugar will sweeten this
bitter crime you support. You are not a violent creature.
Would you whip men the way you saw your donkey
brother whipped?"

"Horse," interjected the baboon, "this bear is trying to
trick you. She is trying to put the bit back in your mouth."

"No!" roared the bear. "I hate bits!"

"There," the baboon pointed to the flight manual

the bear had been reading. "That book is full of animal training and torture! You saw for yourself how this bear was making the dog fetch the stick over and over."

"The baboon is lying!" said the bear.

The horse, in some mental conflict, turned a circle.

And then the baboon, to everyone's surprise, leapt upon his back and began stroking his neck.

"The *bear* is lying," cooed the baboon. "Listen to me and the crow. Right, crow? The Bird Gods speak the truth!"

"Praise to The Egg," cawed the crow, adding to the horse's confusion.

"Horse," pleaded the bear, "will you change your vote?"

But the horse would not. Soothed by the baboon, he stopped turning circles and lay down in the shady grass by the hull of the yacht.

"Praise to The Egg," cried the crow. "Now the sky votes."

"In a minute," said the cat, looking at the horse, who was already half asleep beneath the baboon's clever massaging fingers. "I could nap, too." The cat yawned. "We'll carry on after."

And the cat turned her own circle and lay down to sleep.

The dog wanted to disagree but was also inclined to nap in the warm afternoon sunshine. All the animals, in fact, were rather sleepy, as animals often are.

"But," said the bear, "we have this important vote to make! Lives depend on it!"

"After siesta," purred the cat.

The bear, seeing she would not win the argument, lay down, too.

And with the tally 2–1 in favor of humanity's survival, the animals all drifted off to sleep.

Chapter 7

It is well known that animals dream.

Crows have an especially rich dream life. The more religious crows—like the one at the council—insist that they commune with extinct creatures in their dreams. They claim to have learned much from dinosaurs, and especially from krakens, which went extinct just before The Calamity. Apparently dream krakens told the crows of their battles with ships and sharks and whales, of the deepest kelp forests where they birthed their young, and of kraken operas.

This narrator, for one, is skeptical.

But whether the crows communicate with the dead or

not, their dreams are of historical import. For that afternoon, after siesta, the crow raised his wings up above his head and cleared his throat and said:

"*Caaw!* I dreamed the vote!"

The bear rolled her eyes, but the crow didn't care.

"The only true Gods are the Bird Gods, and crows are their messengers. In the beginning, The Egg. From The Egg, the earth. It is known what the humans have done to the earth, to chicks and nests, to all animals. But what have they done to the Bird Gods? Disrespected them? The Calamity is punishment!"

Listening to the crow, the dog became sleepy again. As far back as he could remember, when the birds talked about their religion, he'd gotten sleepy.

The cat, for her part, was wondering how crow might taste. She was often hungry after a nap.

But the baboon yelled: "Praise to the Bird Gods! How do the crows vote?"

The crow didn't answer the question. Instead he said:

"Hear the bird laws! On the full moon, no worms! On the seventh day, attend thy nest! Thou shalt not fly above the mountain, nor below the sea! *Caw caw caw!*"

"What the devil?" asked the dog.

"The crow seems to have flown into some kind of trance," observed the bear.

And indeed, the crow was hopping and spinning, like he was receiving sacred wisdom, or like his claw was stuck in an electrical socket. The cat, who studied bird dances, had never seen one quite like this. It didn't resemble the blue-footed booby foxtrot, nor the zen waltz of the cranes, stately and delicious.

"Caw caw caw caw!"

The crow seemed to be coming out of the trance.

"A new bird law!" said the crow, returning to his senses. "If you do not eat the humans . . ."

The crow, a ham, paused.

"Well," said the dog, "get on with it!"

". . . the humans will eat you!" said the crow.

"Praise to the Bird Gods," shouted the baboon. "How do you vote?"

"Humans are a danger to The Egg," said the crow. "Kill them all!"

Chapter 8

The bear updated the tally on the tree.

"Bear," said the cat, "do you think it strange that we few should decide the future of all mankind? What if there are other creatures who would like to join in the vote? Perhaps even right now, watching us from beneath the ship, creatures like . . . a *mouse*?"

The cat flicked her ears at the base of the yacht and the animals looked over.

Indeed, there was a mouse, carefully poking his snout into the sunlight.

"Trespasser!" shouted the baboon. "The council is full!"

"Baboon, my friend," said the cat, "no need to shout. Come, mouse, you are welcome. No animal invited to the council shall harm another. This is the law."

The mouse crept out from beneath the yacht.

"No mouse votes!" cried the baboon. "The mouse was not invited!"

"No one is saying so," said the cat. "Let's just hear what it has to say. It must have a reason to approach us here. Speak, mouse."

The mouse, standing on his hind legs, spoke in a proud mouse voice:

"I speak on behalf of the absent council member."

The mouse bowed and flourished his tail.

"I speak also on behalf of all mice and smaller mammals. I speak for the two thousand two hundred and twenty-seven species of rodents, none of whom were invited to this council. We wonder, why this insult?

Did we not suffer in The Calamity? Have we not been involved with humans since they lived by nut and berry gathering? As though mice, rats, squirrels, prairie dogs, gerbils, chinchillas, porcupines, voles, and mighty capy-baras were not living beneath their homes . . ."

"Enough, rodent," sneered the baboon. "What have you come to say?"

"The seventh council member is delayed. He will arrive at sunset. And: the small mammals vote in favor of humanity."

This caused an uproar, for, as the baboon had noted, the mouse had not been invited to vote in the council. All voiced an opinion, some in favor of counting the mouse's vote, some against. The horse whinnied, just to be part of the noise.

And then the cat pounced.

It was done in an instant, though there was much to see. The cat's shoulder blades rising. Her whiskers in the breeze, the twitch of her ears, the widening of her golden eyes. She was airborne.

The mouse, terrified. In his mouse brain, all signals fir-ing. Adrenaline flooded his pea-sized heart. His eyes wid-ened. He tried to flee, but too late. The cat's paw stunned him, a claw pierced his delicate skin. The cat delivered a neck bite, severing the mouse's spine.

The cat gulped down the mouse.

After a moment of silence, the uproar among the animals redoubled.

The cat licked a drop of blood from her paw.

"You've broken the rules of the council," shouted the baboon. "The seventh council member will kill us!"

"Curses on egg crackers!" cawed the crow.

"I have broken no rules," said the cat, repressing a belch. "As my baboon friend says, that mouse was not invited and spoke for no one. I was hungry. And"—she raised her tail straight up, against further objection—"if the seventh council member has a problem, he can take it up with me."

"Classic cat behavior," muttered the dog.

"Now," continued the cat, "there is nothing more difficult than changing an animal's mind. But I will say, in case I can change yours: humans are more useful to us outside our bellies than in. Consider: how many more years will you live? Five? Ten at the most? For myself, I know I shall be dead in no more than ten years—and that would make me a fortunate cat indeed. Remember, humans are dangerous. Why risk the few years we have in hunting them? So that our children might not be endangered by some unpredictable *future* Calamity? What children? My kittens all died in the *last* Calamity."

The cat paused, twitched her whiskers.

"Remember this, too," she said, "humans were *good* for cats. Not for the big kitties, the lions and tigers and so on. I sympathize. But for house cats, and city cats—the time of man was a rich time for us. There was a certain . . .

symbiosis. Not unlike, I must admit, that between man and dog—*n'est-ce pas*, dog?"

And here the cat slyly winked at the dog.

"Well, well, I . . ." the dog stuttered, embarrassed at the association.

The cat now burped quietly and continued. "Domestication was not so bad," she said. "I recall milk in porcelain plates, sunlit cushions high above their cities. I too am saddened by what men have done to the earth. But what arrogance to think we can simply kill all the remaining men! Where did we get this idea? Because the animals of these particular nearby forests have told us that there are only a few men left? But what of the rest of the earth? On the islands of the ocean, in the far reaches of the north, do you think there are no more men? That these men here truly are the last of their kind?"

"Yes!" cried the baboon. "This is known by all the animals. All the animals!"

The cat shook her head, knowing as she did that it was useless to argue with this baboon.

"It is better," said the cat, "to accept what cannot be changed, and pee on it. Cats were not made for one life or another, nor were baboons or bears or horses. Nor, I'm sure, were men. It seems to me rather too much trouble to surround the men and kill them. Why strive for such empty power? Baboon, do you wish for power? Crow, do you?"

"All praise to the nest!" cawed the crow.

"I think," continued the cat, "the baboon has not thought through his plan to kill the humans. I think he has been carried away in the excitement."

Here the cat turned away from the scowling baboon. In particular, she appealed to the horse and crow.

"My fellow creatures, the baboon will not lead you to safety from humans. I think, instead, this baboon will flee at the first sign of danger and will, when it suits him, betray us all. Notice that he carries a bell and a bag. He who hates the humans most is most like them. Remember too, as different as they seem, as horrible as their behavior may have been, *humans are animals*. Whatever they say, whatever they do, whatever Calamities they create upon the earth, each individually is interested in surviving and mating. That is *it*. When I hear the howl of the tomcat, I strut into the moonlight. Same for humans."

"No," shouted the baboon. "Humans are different from animals! The cat is lying!"

"So," the cat continued, "I vote for my own survival. I do not vote for rushing a camp of humans who have probably already built various devices for killing crows and horses and bears and cats in the time that they've had to regroup. I say: don't trust the primates. The cats vote to leave humanity alone."

"No! No!" snarled the baboon. "This is the wrong vote! You betrayed me, cat! We had a deal!"

And with a great roar the baboon rushed the cat, intending, it seemed, to rip her apart.

Chapter 9

We shall leave, for a moment, this scene of impending violence between cat and baboon. But we shall not travel far.

Down the promontory, at the edge of the forest where the humans made their small camp, lived a large tribe of mice. News had already returned to them of their emissary's death at the council, and now the mice were in their own council, discussing the matter.

Consensus was: something had to be done about this cat.

One might quibble over whether or not the mouse had been invited to vote, but the spirit of the agreement had surely been violated. An animal had been eaten at the council. And going forward, they must secure themselves against further attack from what was an unusually cruel and dangerous cat.

In a cavernous burrow beneath an oak tree, the mice debated their response.

"We must ally ourselves with the dogs and horses!"

"We must build a trap!"

"We must ask the seventh council member to avenge our fallen brother!"

And so on. After some time, a young but quite well-regarded mouse stood up with a proposal.

"Let us sneak up on the cat in her sleep," he said, "and tie a bell around her neck. I have taken one from the humans."

Several of this young mouse's acolytes emerged from within the tunnel complex dragging a shiny bell, much like the one so beloved by the baboon.

"When it rings, the cat shall never be able to pounce on us again!"

The gathered mice applauded this idea roundly and congratulated the speaker on his wisdom.

But a frizzy furred ancient mouse was not so sure.

"And who," he asked, "will bell the cat?"

A long moment of silence.

Finally, the young mouse who suggested the idea spoke up, huffily.

"*I* will bell the cat," he said, "tonight or in the morning, whenever the cat next goes to sleep."

At this there was more applause from the gathered mice. And, to their surprise, some additional, slower, higher-pitched applause.

It was coming from the burrow entrance, from some unexpected guests.

Clap . . . clap . . . clap.

The mice quieted, and looked:

Cockroaches.

"Mammals," the spokesroach said. "You mammals, thinking about mammals. To hell with your little bell. We have a better plan. . . ."

And he began to explain.

Listening to the roaches, the frizzy old mouse wished he knew history better, had some guidance greater than his own limited experience. Were roaches to be trusted? Not so many generations before, in the human cities, roaches and mice lived tail to shell. But the old mouse realized he'd never had a real conversation with a roach. He didn't know what it was like to have hundreds of children, or to walk upside down. But mice and roaches, he thought, must have things in common. Fear of being stomped by humans. And, did he recall correctly that cats will eat a roach sometimes? Monstrous creatures, cats, they would eat anything, . . . and this old mouse was a bit hungry himself just then. A blackberry, yes, that would be the thing, or even, if there were no berries, some of that dead worm he recalled seeing . . .

"Sir," one of the younger mice was saying. "Sir?"

The frizzy old mouse snapped out of his reverie.

The younger mice wanted to know:

What did he think of the cockroaches' proposal?

Chapter 10

Back on the cliff, the baboon was bull-rushing the cat. But:

The dog intervened!

Leapt between the two, bowled the baboon over. Saved the cat's life! He was a highly trained military creature, after all.

Still, it was a very close thing—the baboon had nearly got the cat by the tail, might have ripped it right off.

The cat, hissing, crouched behind the bear.

Regaining his paws, the dog snarled at the baboon, who, baring his teeth, howled in frustration. The horse was so stunned he turned three circles.

"You betrayed me, cat!" yowled the baboon.

The cat only hissed back. The dog was still barking. The horse whimpering. The crow cawing. The baboon furiously slapped the ground and gnashed his teeth and rang his bell.

Finally, the bear could take the noise no longer and let out a great roar, quieting the rest.

"Enough, baboon! What are you doing? No animal is to hurt another at the council!"

The dog, out of breath, stopped barking. "All dogs accounted for?! Alamo? Biscuits? General Bill?"

Unanswered, the dog started barking again. The crow flapped down beside him.

"The battle is over. Over! *Caw!*"

"That cat ate the mouse," said the baboon to the bear, accusingly. "Maybe I'll eat the cat."

"But, as the cat said," noted the bear, slowly, "the mouse wasn't really invited. . . ."

Even as the bear said this, she realized she didn't believe the argument the cat had made. It did not seem right for the cat to have eaten that mouse. And then the bear remembered what the baboon had said just before he attacked. . . .

"What was that," the bear asked, "you were saying about a deal?"

"The cat and I had agreed to vote together," said the baboon, glad to betray the cat.

The bear shook her head and sighed. She looked at the cat with reproach, but the cat only shrugged.

✦

This historian has been unable to verify what passed between the cat and the baboon. Sadly, we must proceed with fuzzy variables, unknowns.

This is inevitable, of course. The task before us is to live with limited information. Perhaps the baboon and the cat had simply misunderstood each other. Perhaps the cat tricked the baboon, or vice versa. The answer is obscure, not to be found in my hundreds of hours of interviews with baboons and cats; nor in cat archives, where this historian pored over their nearly indecipherable scratchings; nor among the singing storyteller baboons, in their banana skin epics. History will simply not give up her secrets on this matter.

We *do* know, however, that when the animals had calmed down after the fracas, the baboon proceeded to make his case.

He was himself well versed in the history of humanity's poor decisions. More convincing, perhaps, than the cat expected.

✦

The baboon stalked among the animals. Even the bear was uneasy. An angry baboon is dangerous, and the cat had only just escaped with her life.

"Stupid animals!" said the baboon. "I won't waste primate time on a speech to stupid animals. I vote to kill the humans."

"Baboon, why?" said the bear. "You were closer to them than any of us."

"Why?" Here the baboon dropped his voice. "Closer? They cut down the forest and burned the plain. They poured poison in the ocean and sprayed it in the sky. They paved grasslands. They built cages and locked us up. They cut us open; they put chains around our necks and forced us to dance. They hunted us for sport. The bear says some of them wanted balance, but the bear knows most of them didn't! They wanted only to stuff their bellies with our flesh and spray their poisons so they could use their *devices*. And they caused The Calamity. You think I am some baboon who lived in the forests and does not know men. But I was in their university. They kept me in a laboratory. They did not speak grak, but they knew we were not dumb, that we animals were not like plants and rocks. They knew. We spoke in sign language. They watched me paint. You animals have sympathy for man. You think man is part of the balance. What would man do? Man would kill all of us. They even kill their own kind, millions of men, killed in wars. No baboons ever did this. No bears, no cats, no dogs. Only men. This is *unnatural*. We must kill and eat them."

All of this was not, strictly, accurate. Baboons do indeed kill (and eat) their own kind, though not on the scale of man. In any case, the baboon was just getting warmed up—but then, he was interrupted.

It was another animal's call, enormously loud. It contained the alto of a thousand bugles and the *basso profundo* of a whale's heartbeat. But this was no giant marching band or whale.

The earth beneath the animals' feet trembled; the air around them warmed. The call went on for several seconds. None of the animals had ever heard anything like it. It came from over the edge of the cliff.

"Eggs have mercy," cawed the crow, and recited his favorite prayer, Our Finch, under his breath.

"The seventh council member . . ." said the cat.

"Mark my vote, bear!" said the baboon. "Kill the humans!"

The tally for humanity stood at 3–3. And the seventh council member had arrived.

Chapter 11

It is the historian's business to separate fact from fiction. Still, we must recognize some biases are inescapable. Even the most circumspect tortoise scholars, even whales with their extraterrestrial purrviews, have the prejudices of their time and pod. I often think that historians with shorter life spans capture the essence of history with greater grace and insight. I direct you, for example, to the books of cricket wisdom.

Humanity, however, as has been noted, never spoke grak, and so could not learn animal histories. They were therefore blinkered to some realities that were obvious throughout the Animal Kingdom. Chief among these: the existence of so-called "mythical" beasts.

What was it about humanity that prevented them from admitting the existence, for example, of the yeti? How many yetis did they need to see? Some of our less sympathetic thinkers have suggested that humanity only believes in animals it captures or kills. A grim explanation but not entirely out of character, I'm afraid.

The yetis didn't mind, mostly, though there were a few outliers, romantics who would have liked exchange of one kind or another. I am reminded of a doomed affair between a yeti and a human in the Jharlang valley. The former had rescued the latter from a rockslide, but the obstacles of their respective cultures overpowered their affections. Within the local cave complex, the yetis were concerned—rightly—that humanity would kill and skin them, or concoct some gruesome use for their livers, as they had done with geese. (Yetis and geese share an aesthetic tradition.) The human in question understood their concern and swore he would never return to his village. But his yeti lover was so incensed at the insult from her fellows that she stormed from the cave complex, enraged, and was banished. The two of them could not, obviously, live in the human village. And so they lived out their days among the highest peaks.

But I digress.

On hearing the call from beyond the cliff, the animals looked to the sky for the seventh council member:

The "mythical" creatures had elected to send a dragon as their representative.

But there was no dragon to be seen.

The cat had a keener sense of hearing than the other creatures. She walked to the edge of the cliff. It seemed to her that the call they'd heard had come from down below, rather than up above. She looked over the edge.

Far beneath, where the waves crashed white and foamy on the rocks, she saw the creature who had made the enormous noise. There were several names for her kind, but most often the creature was called *goda*.

Like all goda, this goda had both paws and fins and was covered in black fur. Her face, the only hairless part of her body, was the color of fire coral. She was about dog sized, and eight hundred years old.

The cat looked down at the goda, and the goda looked up at the cat.

Chapter 12

"I don't see a dragon," said the baboon, searching the sky, panic in his voice.

"If the mythical beasts said a dragon will join us," said the dog, "a dragon will join us."

"This council was a bad idea." The baboon's voice wobbled. "We should never have met. The dragon will eat us!"

"Calm yourself," said the bear. "We're civil with one another. We build trust. So will the dragon."

The baboon spat another great wad of phlegm, nearly at the dog's paws. The dog thought to himself: *Something is wrong with that baboon's lungs.* He remembered visiting a veterinarian as a pup, when he had an infection. Every breath had been clogged, like having your snout stuck in the mud. There was all the unpleasantness of the sterile white room and the stranger poking him, but the humans had been telling the truth. The vet helped him breathe. He might never have been a soldier if it hadn't been for that vet. . . .

"Baboon," said the dog, "do you know about vets? Some of the humans are very good at healing animals."

"I wish," said the horse, who had been thinking hard since the goda's call, "that they had sent a unicorn."

The cat, returning from the cliff, informed the council: "It's not a dragon."

"Don't trust a word this cat says," said the baboon. "She's—"

Before the baboon could carry on with what surely would have been a nasty string of invective, the goda arrived. With her strong paws she had climbed the side of the cliff and was now standing before the animals, her curly hair rippling in the breeze, the dusk light reflected in her dark eyes. Her voice was like rocks crashing against each other underwater.

"Greetings," she said.

✦

The animals of the council fell silent. They did not know many "mythical" beasts. No creature, however, impresses cockroaches, and a great many of them were watching the goda, too. The weeds and grasses and shrubs around the cliff were in fact dense with cockroaches, all of whom watched and listened to see how the vote would go, as they groomed each other and nibbled on the available organic matter. The cliff was also dense with mice and rats, peering from burrows, observing the proceedings.

Most of the animals at the council were so interested in the goda that they did not notice the extra rodent scent on the breeze, which had strengthened as the sun was setting.

The baboon, however, was well aware of the watchers.

The baboon had, after all, recruited the bugs and rodents into a plot.

Such terrible violence among these animals.

Among all animals.

I do not like even to continue with this history.

But it is the duty of the historian to face the hideous facts, and violence is one.

Some weather was coming in off the horizon.

✦

The moment the lion takes down the gazelle is not good for the gazelle. The tendons rip, the blood spurts, the gazelle's consciousness returns to the void or perhaps moves on to the heavenly savannahs. I have always been most sympathetic to the herbivores. Sometimes I think that the worst mistake animals ever made was evolving out of the antediluvian ooze. What a tranquil, nutrient-rich time that must have been.

Alas, there is no turning back the evolutionary clock. We evolved to eat each other.

And at this moment in our chronicle, as the goda prepared to cast a vote on behalf of dragons and the other "mythical" beasts, the animals teetered on the brink of carnage and betrayal.

The baboons and cockroaches and mice had entered into a brutal alliance. If the vote did not go the way they wanted, if the council concluded that humanity should be left alone, they would swarm. They would kill and eat the pro-human animals, and then move on to the humans.

Such a conspiracy was not unprecedented. The great auk councils of centuries prior had been plagued by intrigues, though the root cause of their extinction, of course, was humanity. The destruction of the Maya followed a particularly turbulent political season among the animals of the Yucatán. A human disease had wiped out a great number of the creatures in the nearby rain forest, and the council convened, voted, and subsequently carried out a campaign of immense destruction on the people of those Mayan cities. Carried them off screaming into the jungle, devoured them in their beds. Nothing left of the whole civilization but empty cities, bones, and panther scat.

But I digress again.

A million roaches, watching.

✦

"Greetings," said the bear, respectfully, to the goda.

"Bird blessings on you," said the crow.

The goda nodded to each in turn.

The dog, perhaps because he'd spent so much time among men, was most surprised of all by the goda. He could not place her particular scent.

He also found it quite fetching. Something about the goda reminded him of a shih tzu he'd loved long ago.

"Welcome to headquarters," the dog blurted out.

The goda turned her dark-eyed gaze upon him, and the dog scratched himself, drooling.

"Would you like some sugar?" said the horse, nodding at the chewed-up box.

The goda bowed again, slightly.

The animals waited to hear what she would say. A few seconds, then a few more.

As the time passed it seemed that the goda was looking deeply into each one of them, considering. In actuality, the goda moved very, very slowly because she was eight hundred years old.

The baboon, impatient, twirled the fur on his head in such a way that he now had small tufts pointing in every direction. Finally, he could take the silence no longer:

"Where is the dragon?" he asked.

The goda looked up into the sky, and all the animals followed her gaze. But there was no dragon, only the cooling blue and pink and yellow of the sunset. When they looked back down, the goda was looking over the bear's tally. She lifted one of her paws.

All around them, the rodents and roaches crouched, watching the baboon for the signal, ready to charge.

And the goda marked her vote.

The baboon, triumphant, threw a hairy arm into the air and hooted with pleasure.

All around, roaches and rodents relaxed.

"Wait, but, please," said the bear, "goda, why? The humans venerate you. They worship dragons, why . . . ?"

But the goda was already walking to the edge of the cliff.

"Please," said the bear, "where is the mercy? There is no evil in nature. We must not do this thing!"

The goda stopped and turned and asked the animals a question. But it didn't sound like a question.

"How," she said in her great undersea voice, "do you get a goose out of a bottle?"

And then she dove over the side of the cliff.

Chapter 13

The bear and the dog rushed to the side of the cliff, but there was no sign of the goda.

"Look there," said the dog, "eleven o'clock, a, a, an unidentified . . ."

A glowing orb sped away beneath the waves.

The dog couldn't explain how he knew, but somehow he knew—it was the goda. (Knowledgeable sea creatures confirm this "lighting up" is common goda behavior.) His heart skipped a beat within the furry confines of his chest.

"Wait!" he cried out.

But the goda, with her lovely curly fur, was gone.

The dog looked to the bear with unconcealable sadness. The last light of day was blue; the stony smell of rain blew in off the sea.

"You did well to save the cat," said the bear.

"But we lost the vote," said the dog. "We lost . . ."

The bear frowned. "We must have hope," she said, slowly, "that the animals will come to their senses. Come."

They walked back to the council as the first distant thunder rolled.

"Come out," the baboon was shouting, "show yourselves!"

He rang his bell, and the rodents and the roaches emerged.

"What's this?" asked the bear. "Were you all watching, all the time?"

"Down with the mammals!" came the collective cockroach response.

Fat drops of rain began to fall.

"No time for questions, bear," said the baboon. "The vote is over. This is a war council now. We must return to our species with this news. We meet here again in two days, and then kill the humans. Terrible humans, terrible! The council is adjourned! For victory!"

The baboon rang his bell again, but its note was lost in the rain. He stowed it away and knuckled off, followed by a mass of roaches and rodents.

"Blows around The Egg, a bad wind," cawed the

crow. He spread his wings and stepped into the air, circling higher and higher until he was lost to the other animals.

The horse sniffed at the yellow box, now empty of sugar, then turned to the dog.

"Sugar cubes? Carrots?"

"You just voted to end humanity, you bloody imbecile!"

"Easy, dog," said the bear. "No, horse, no sugar cubes. The council is over."

The horse looked blankly from bear to dog and back again.

". . . And so you should go, now. Tell the other horses."

The horse shook his head and trotted off through the rain, into the falling darkness.

The cat, dry in the cockpit of the helicopter, looked at the two creatures who remained. The losers of the vote, wet and despondent.

"Come," said the cat, "I know a cave where we can shelter from this storm."

"I must return to the pack," said the dog. He had never visited a cat den before and didn't want to now.

"Dog," said the cat, hopping down from the helicopter into the wet grass. "A storm is coming. It is not a good time to return to the pack. There are even bones in this cave. You are welcome. Bear, will you come?"

The bear grunted in assent, and together they departed.

"Blast," said the dog, watching them walk off. "I'll

be a stew before I go to some cat's stinking cat hole. Orders are orders, a vote is a vote, we're soldiers, not politicians, dammit. Hate the way it's gone but nothing to do and that's that."

The dog saluted no one in particular, determined to make the long walk back to his pack.

Just then a great crash of thunder broke over his head. Lightning forked across the sky.

"Wait, wait!" shouted the dog after the cat and bear. "I'm coming!"

And he ran off after them.

Chapter 14

The cat's cave was down at the base of the cliff. A curtain of glowing Spanish moss obscured the entrance. The bear was no botanist, but she knew it was the post-Calamity moss. Many plant species had mutated during The Calamity—certain forests had turned to plastic—and one of the more common mutations was the glow. A bright turquoise, pulsing in the veins of the moss. The bear followed the cat and dog through the glowing curtain.

The cave smelled of old moss. The stone walls muffled the sound of the rain.

"Bloody rotten weather out there," said the dog, shaking himself off. He wouldn't admit it, but this seemed like a good spot the cat had found. Dry and warm and, sure enough, there was a pile of bones against the wall.

"Cat," the bear said, "what happened between you and the baboon?"

The dog walked over to the pile of bones. Not clear exactly who they'd been, but they looked tasty enough. He was just leaning in for a long flat one, perhaps some kind of scapula, when the pile exploded outward, bones clattering.

The dog yelped and leapt back.

A trio of moles tumbled elegantly from the pile of bones. Flipping and cartwheeling, they landed, with perfect stillness, in a triangle around the dog.

Soft and velvety though they were, they seemed rather dangerous.

"What in the blazes?"

"Not to worry, dog," said the cat. "They're friends."

The moles, as one, bowed to the cat. The cat bowed back.

The bear studied the moles. When she was a cub, she had worked on a film playing the pet of a warlord. It had been a formative role in her artistic development—she had realized that the acts that brought her the most joy did the same for the audience. Now her mind returned to the film, but not because of artistic development. These moles reminded her of some of the *characters* the humans had played. . . . What were they called? Dressed in black, creeping on rooftops, masks . . . They disappeared in smoke, carried curved swords and nunchukas and throwing stars . . . The word was on the tip of her tongue. . . .

The three moles sat cross-legged against the wall of the cave.

"We feared we'd lose the vote," said the cat, trailing off. "But hoped . . ."

The cat seemed suddenly very tired. Then she gathered herself, swishing her tail.

"Now," said the cat, "we have much work to do. These moles have found a way into the human's camp."

"Cat," said the bear, "what are you talking about?"

"Diplomacy has failed," said the cat. "The baboons

are out of control. They play on the other animals' fears about humans for their own ends. You heard yourself, bear, the lies that baboon told. But we have a backup plan. Humans are too useful for us to let them be slaughtered."

"But we have a system, a tradition," said the bear. "We've lost the vote. We must abide by the results. What do you think, dog?"

"I'm a soldier. Politics isn't my business."

"So you think the humans should all be killed and eaten?" said the cat.

"I think it's a damn shame, but orders are orders."

"When the orders are unjust, it's your duty to disobey."

The dog grunted.

The cat said: "We're going to warn the humans—"

"Mutiny!" barked the dog. "The baboons will never stand for it!"

"We're going to warn the humans," the cat pressed on, "so they can escape extinction."

"You saw the bugs with that baboon," said the bear. "Even if the crows don't see us first, the bugs will report our movements to the baboons. We'll never make it to the humans without their knowing. And even if we did, the humans would never be able to escape the other animals banded against them."

The cat fixed the bear with a stare through the darkness.

"What do you propose, bear? Let them die, abandon hope?"

The bear was so tired. Since The Calamity, the seasons had become disordered. She'd tried to argue; she'd tried to teach the dog new thinking. All for nothing. The bear was feeling that it had been a long time since she'd hibernated. And this was such a pleasant, dry cave; perhaps she would just lie down for a few months and let all the trouble with the humans and the vote take its course. . . .

"It's impossible," said the bear, slumping. "Humanity is finished."

"I have a plan," said the cat.

Silence in the cave. Against the wall, the dangerous moles sat in absolute stillness.

"Well?!" said the dog. "What's the plan?!"

The future balanced upon the edge of a cat's claw.

"The moles have found a tunnel from this cave to the human camp," said the cat. "We can warn the humans and be away before the other council species find out."

"But even if we get in and out," said the dog, "how would we warn them? They never read nature's signs before."

"One of them," said the cat, "speaks grak."

The bear and dog looked at each other in disbelief.

Silence in the cave.

"A squirrel heard an old woman in the camp," the cat went on. "They call her a witch."

"And you believe this . . . secret squirrel?" asked the dog.

"I do."

The dog frowned. This notion that an old human lady in the camp spoke grak was far-fetched, at best. What would the pack say? He'd been sent to represent them and report back the decision of the council, and now he was being drawn into some . . . feline conspiracy. He looked to the bear for guidance, but the bear turned away and lay her head down on the cool stone.

"Bear," said the cat, "you can't turn away and ignore this. What of your speech at the council? Were you only *acting*?"

The bear wondered: *Am I?* She cast her memory back over her life. Her mother. A silver salmon leaping. She was so young when she was captured. The humans who were always gentle with her. *What a good bear.* Did it mean nothing?

"Bear," insisted the cat, "what of loyalty?"

The dog, listening, was surprised at the question. Cats weren't loyal.

"I *am* loyal," said the bear, deliberately. "I am loyal to the vote."

One of the dangerous moles rose silently from his place on the floor. He seemed to flow rather than walk through the turquoise gloom. Equidistant from bear and cat, he stopped and held in the air: a cocoon.

The first cracks showed along its side.

"What's this?" asked the bear.

The mole gave a brief nod, then secreted the cocoon away and returned to his cross-legged pose against the wall.

"It's a timer," explained the cat. "When a butterfly emerges from that cocoon, the moles' access tunnels to the witch's camp will collapse. We're running out of time; we must go." The cat caught the eyes of the dog and winked. "You say you're loyal to the vote, bear. In that case, let's have another. We vote on whether to warn the humans."

The cat raised her paw. "I vote aye. And these moles' vows prevent them from voting."

One of the moles rose, bowed, and sat again.

"Dog?"

The dog looked over his shoulder, but there was no pack to guide him.

"Dog," purred the cat, approaching, close enough that the dog's congested nose was filled with cat stink, "thank you for protecting me from the baboon."

"Just my job," the dog said automatically.

"This is the moment," purred the cat, "when hero dogs rise up. . . ."

To the bear, it looked like the cat was hypnotizing the dog.

"The moment," continued the cat, "when they are

best friends not only to man, but to *all* animals. Guard dog, sheepdog, Seeing Eye dog, attack dog. Rescue dog. This is their moment. *They* are the kind of dogs that a . . . *goda* would fall in love with."

"Well, I, what, I mean, love, there's no, not at . . ."

"How do you vote, dog?"

The dog wagged his tail.

Chapter 15

The bear could have left. The vote in the cave, instigated by the cat, was nonbinding.

Instead, after the dog voted in favor of warning the humans, the bear stuck around. She joined the cat, the dog, and the three moles on their quest.

I wonder whether she would have made the same decision if she had known what lay ahead.

Every vote requires courage. Not the kind you need to battle mutated tunnel slugs—though that's important, too. No, the kind of courage that allows you to look the slugs in the eye and say: let's decide on this together. In the belief that a calamitous slug is, finally, not so different

from a bear, or dog. Idealistic? Naïve? Perhaps. Perhaps the act of writing history is idealistic, too. . . .

But I digress.

The moles led the way to the back of the cave, to a mole-sized hole.

It slanted down into darkness. One after another, the moles flipped inside and disappeared.

"Who planned this mission, cat?" said the dog, sniffing the hole. "I can barely fit. Need the ratter squad for a job like this. And the bear's not going to fit in there at all—she's a bear! Classic cat plann—"

The cat disappeared into the hole.

"Well, that's bloody something, isn't it," the dog

barked at the bear. "All this windup about heroism and a vote and now the cat leaves us off mission, behind the wire like a bunch of pups."

The bear sniffed at the hole. She smelled something . . . chemical. She remembered it from certain action sequences she'd shot, but couldn't quite place it. . . . She sniffed again. . . .

WHMUPF! KABANG! SHRUUSSH!

The floor around them shuddered and collapsed in on itself.

The bear and dog, sliding at high speed down a steeply slanted tunnel and then, falling through space: a vast cavern.

Then the sharp embrace of icy water. The dog gasped as he went under.

✦

The subterranean salt-lake cavern into which the dog and bear had fallen was of unusual historical significance.

In this cavern, philosopher bat kings had ruled over what is universally regarded as the bat midnight (or noonday, depending on your circadian rhythm). Their lengthy reign saw the emergence of the sonar epics, cave portraiture, and guano statuaries which would influence so much artistic life throughout that biosphere.

Humans, of course, had no idea this was going on beneath their stubby toes. The philosopher bat kings tried frequently to initiate contact, but to no avail. Their bat kingdom was eventually destroyed by the white-nose fungus that presaged The Calamity. Even in death the bat philosophers were graceful. At dusk when we hear strains of sonar death sagas in the squeaking of the rare survivors, even insects are moved. Though no death is agreeable, among some insects, death in the jaws of a bat is considered ideal.

The dog spluttered to the surface.

The cavern was so enormous he could not see where it ended. But from darkness he emerged into light: everywhere he looked, cool green phosphorescence. The water all around him glowed and swirled. The bear was some lengths to shore already. The dog paddled after and dragged himself, shivering, onto the rocky bank. The cat and the dangerous moles were waiting.

"Apologies for the bath," said the cat.

The bear, though she happened to like swimming in cold water, shook dry in a great, unhappy spray. The dog, panting and puffing, did likewise.

"Cat," the dog said, "we need to *communicate*. Comms is the key to any mission, and that break in the chain was an opsec disaster! You keep at it like this, I'll have your tail court-martialed."

The cat only licked a paw.

"Which way now, cat?" growled the bear, rather threateningly.

The cat pointed with her tail down the shoreline toward the cavern wall, against which stood a giant boulder, twice as wide and tall as the bear. "Behind that boulder."

"Behind that boulder?" asked the bear. "How did the moles get past it? It's solid rock all around there!"

The moles whispered in the cat's ear.

"Yes, it is strange," said the cat. "The boulder wasn't there before."

"Then what in the blazes are we going to do?" said the dog. "Are we stuck down—"

"ANIMALS, BEGONE!"

A powerful voice echoed off the cavern walls, interrupting. It seemed to come from every direction.

Tail to tail to tail, the cat and dog and bear braced

themselves for attack. The bear reared up on her hind legs, the cat hissed, the dog growled. The moles vanished in a cloud of purple smoke.

"**APOLOGIZE!**" echoed the booming voice.

"Who's there?" cried the cat. "We mean no trespass and would talk with whatever animals are here."

"I think it's coming from the water," said the bear.

Just offshore, the water churned and sucked. Something was rising up.

"There!"

High on the walls of the cavern, the three moles aimed their poison dart blowguns at the roiling water, prepared to fire.

From the froth emerged a mighty head, silver and white. Such a head as the bear had never seen. It was massive. Cave kelp hung from its teeth. Green slime sloughed off its scales. And this fierce creature, a giant cave lizard, fixed the animals with its unblinking eyes.

"Greetings," said the cat.

"**Why do you enter the bat cavern?**"

"We're on our way to a human camp aboveground," said the cat.

"**The bat cavern is the sacred homeland of the bats.**"

With astonishing speed for a creature so large, the lizard boiled up out of the water and touched down on the shore between the animals and the tunnel. On land, the lizard was even bigger than they'd imagined, three times the size of the bear. It could clearly eat them all up.

"Apologies," said the bear, "we did not know—"

"**You did not know that the above-grounders infected and oppressed us?**"

"Well, we . . ."

"**We're not going to listen to your above-splaining. To your bipedalist hate speech! Only bats can know the truth!**"

"My friend," said the dog, "what bats are you talking about?"

And indeed, the dog had the right of it. There was not a bat to be seen anywhere in the cavern.

"**WE ARE BATS!**" roared the lizard. "**SQUEAK ON!**"

"Squeak on," echoed the bear, trying to get in the swing of things.

But this was evidently the wrong thing to say.

The giant lizard flicked its tongue out in anger and screeched, a horrible sound.

"**Who gave you the right to squeak on?**" he demanded.

"I, I, I meant no disrespect," said the bear. "I—"

"**It's not enough that you invade our cave and infect our ancestors. Now you have to steal our language?**"

"Steal *whose* language!?" barked the dog. "You're not even a bat!"

The lizard's eyes went wide as headlights. He reared back. Curved rows of teeth in green bio-light.

The dangerous moles, clinging to the cavern wall high above, assessed the situation. In their mole hearts, chips of ice. Campaign after campaign, mission after mission, killing after killing, these moles had abided by a code. *Darkness above light, loyalty above death, tunnel forever.* In bygone times such moles had served badger lords and turned the tide of certain conflicts. It was a secretive tradition but robust; their legend spread. In The Calamity, however, these moles had lost their masters. In their wanderings they had fallen in with the cat.

And now they would watch this giant lizard, who thought he was a bat, eat the dog.

Chapter 16

"Please," said the cat, before the lizard could strike. "Forgive my friend. He needs education. He's not awake to the realities of aboveground/underground."

The lizard relaxed his mighty neck. "**We must educate the ignorant.**"

"Please," said the bear, "educate us."

"**They never treated us like animals,**" the lizard began. "**They treated us like machines. Guano-producing machines. In the beginning we didn't mind, humans coming down here, carting it all away. They used to fertilize their** vegetables. But the more they came, the sicker we got. And they didn't care. Other animals danced to the sonar epics. And all the while humanity is coming down and taking our guano, infecting our cave. And one day, I look around and there's only a few hundred of us left. And then fifty. And then just me and my family. And then only me."

The giant lizard shut his scaled eyes and sucked air through serrated teeth.

"I am the last of the bats."

"I'm sorry," said the cat. "That is . . . profound."

"It is the truth."

"Well, look," said the cat, "no animal can make up for what the humans did to you. But the aboveground animals have decided to kill the humans."

"Bats have a different justice."

The lizard was right, of course. Aboveground justice relied on a jury system. Down below, the system was older and depended wholly on judges—typically highly respected female bats (though never members of the royal line). Disputes were resolved rapidly, and nonviolently. Emphasis was on reintegration of the perpetrator into bat society, even in the rare instances of bat-on-bat violence. It was a low-crime society.

(An aside—in the bibliography, you will find reference to the remarkable *Informal Justice in the Midnight*

Kingdom of the Philosopher Bats. A work of both legal theory and anthropology, squeaked by a distinguished, multidisciplinary bat, and translated into grak. I cannot recommend it highly enough—it shaped my own thinking as a legal historian.)

"And a fine system bat justice is," said the cat. "We don't believe in executions either. Which is why we need your help. We were going to go to the human camp, to warn them about the other animals, but that boulder is in the way. Do you know another way out of this cavern?"

"I put the boulder in front of the tunnel."

"But why?" asked the cat.

"There is no respect for bats. We will not tolerate insults from above-grounders, passing through our sacred cavern, using it as they please."

The bear stepped forward.

"Bat," she said, "we apologize for trespassing in your cavern. We didn't know what we were doing—"

"The moles knew," said the lizard, looking about for them.

High against the cavern wall, moles in perfect stillness, camouflaged against dark rock.

"We can't speak for the moles," continued the bear. "But if we don't warn these humans, the rest of the animals are going to kill them. All of them. Their species will go extinct."

"Like mine."

The bear and cat nodded seriously.

"It is a tragedy for any species to go extinct."

"Yes," purred the cat. "Exactly."

The giant lizard picked at a fish head between his teeth.

"How will you warn the humans?"

"There's a human who speaks grak."

"Impossible."

"It's true," said the cat. "The animals of the forest have all heard."

"If this is true, they must know our pain!"

"Yes," said the cat to the bear, "if only we had some creature who could speak of the injustice the humans have perpetrated. Even when they didn't mean to—"

"Yes," agreed the bear, "the way they treated animals like . . . like guano machines."

"They did!" The lizard snarled, and the cavern walls shook with his rage. "I will tell the humans," he declared.

"You?" said the cat slyly.

"Yes! I will testify that the humans killed my bat brothers and bat sisters with their carelessness, with their white-nose fungus. My truth will be heard."

"Squeak on!" said the cat.

"SQUEAK ON!!" roared the lizard. "Bring me to the humans!"

"Would love to," said the cat, "but first, we need to warn them, you see, so they can survive to hear your testimony, and their camp is down the tunnel, on the other side of that boulder. . . ."

"You may pass through the bat kingdom!" said the lizard.

And then he put his scaly shoulders against the boulder.

"Hunhnn . . ."

The boulder shifted.

His vast claws dug into the cavern floor, his scales scratching against the cold stone of the boulder, his black-and-green eyes slit in effort. . . .

"HunhnnnhnAARR!"

And the boulder rolled away, revealing a tunnel, just large enough to fit the bear.

"Now," said the lizard, panting, "go. Quiet as the stars, smooth as the light at dusk, softly as the dew. Like bats. When must I come above-ground to testify?"

"Tomorrow," said the cat, "on the cliff's edge, by the human boat."

The lizard held his front legs up, as though they were bat wings. But, of course, he flew nowhere.

"I will squeak truth to power." The lizard lowered his front legs.

"We thank you. Bear, dog, let's go."

The moles were already ahead of them. Walking away, the dog glanced over his shoulder and saw the lizard slithering back into the frigid salt lake.

Chapter 17

The tunnel stretched out. Soon it was high and wide enough for a locomotive. The animals walked abreast among crystal stalactites.

"Are you really going to call that lizard to . . . testify?" said the bear to the cat.

"I already did," said the cat.

"And you think it will come aboveground?"

"If he does come aboveground, what harm? Let the humans hear from him."

"That lizard is crazy!" barked the dog. "It thinks it's a bat!"

"So?" said the cat.

"So it's a lizard, not a bat!" said the dog. "I think that lizard *ate* all the bats."

"All mammals are evolved from lizards, or some common creature. Let the lizard channel his bat-self."

"Nonsense," said the dog. "What if the lizard said it was a cat? Or a dog? Next you'll want it sleeping in our doghouses. Well I won't have it! It's not right. It wouldn't even *fit* inside a doghouse."

"Pooch," said the cat, "doghouses are human constructions anyway."

"Call me pooch again, cat, see what happens."

The dog growled. This whole mission was cock-eyed, and now the cat was calling him *pooch*. He was not a dog to get offended, but the word *pooch* carried a heavy load. It was impolite, if not shocking, for any animal besides dogs to use it. Humans, of course, not speaking grak, didn't know any better. They didn't know the story. The word carried all the trauma accumulated in one of the darkest periods of dog-cat history.

Pooch originated in ancient Egypt, under the rule of the Cat Pharaohs. At that time, cats had pride of place among the humans. They were worshipped as gods. This was no problem for the dogs until the rise of a particular cat.

Mafdet was the human name for a Cairene street cat who, through a combination of luck, cunning, and snake-killing prowess, ingratiated herself into the pharaoh's court. This particular pharaoh was vain, insecure, eventually insane. Mafdet played on her fears, whispered in her ear. Mafdet's legend says that she was able to speak human languages. This is of course impossible. It is not impossible, however, that a shrewd cat could manipulate a weak human, and this is exactly what Mafdet did.

Which was bad luck for humans, many of whom were forced to carve massive cat heads into stone under the desert sun. It was even worse luck for a particular dog, whom this pharaoh had named *Pooch*. Mafdet and Pooch were, it is said, originally competing for the affection of the pharaoh. But it was no contest. Mafdet framed Pooch for spilled wine on handwoven silks; for turds in the temple; for scaring a favored concubine. And finally:

Mafdet convinced the pharaoh to exile Pooch. But first: torture.

I am reluctant to recount it. The tale comes to us through the hieroglyphs of Mafdet's temple in greater detail than any decent animal could wish to know: a stick thrown just beyond the reach of a chain; Pooch submerged in oils, removed, submerged, and removed; Pooch's nails pulled out; his tail lit on fire. Worse.

In all the depictions, Mafdet looks on calmly. Thereafter the pharaoh proclaimed dogs unclean, and her people began to treat them cruelly, misuse them. At the height of her power, Mafdet might see from Pooch's litter a dog in the street and say, threatening, *Ah, are you in Pooch's pack?* This struck fear into any dog. And so Pooch's name became a byword for cruelty. Rebellious dogs, then and since, have called each other by the name in solidarity, turning the cat's fearful language to their own strength. The sands of the desert, of course, eventually covered Mafdet's temple and all her cruelties. But the word remained.

And so in the tunnel the dog, hearing this word *pooch*, growled.

The cat had not heard the legend of Mafdet. Where the cat came from, *pooch* carried none of that baggage.

The bear, though, knew the history of the word. "You shouldn't use that word, cat," she said.

And the cat, respecting the bear, hearing her tone, wanting to keep the dog on board, said: "I'm sorry, dog, I didn't know the word was so troublesome."

The dog huffed but was mollified.

The animals continued down the tunnel for a while in silence.

Chapter 18

"Cat," said the dog, "how will we find the woman who speaks grak?"

They had been walking through the tunnel for a long time. Periodically, one of the dangerous moles would stop and place his diggers on the tunnel wall, testing for the particular texture, temperature, and vibration that indicated their location.

"We'll find her," said the cat.

"That's not a plan!" said the dog.

"The dog asks a reasonable question, cat," said the bear. "What *is* your plan?"

"The squirrel told me she lives by herself, in a hut near the camp, and that she likes to sing. We'll be able to find her."

The dog and bear reflected on this.

"What if she has a gun?" asked the dog after a moment.

"The squirrels tell me there are no guns in the village."

"Then how have the humans been hunting?" asked the bear.

"They've been foraging," explained the cat. "And, being city people, they're struggling to survive. They can't find berries and don't know which ones are safe to eat. They've barely been able to make fire. They haven't caught a single rabbit with their traps. They've been eating bugs but not the tastiest bugs. They're arguing among themselves. The squirrels think they won't survive the winter."

The moles, leading the way, stopped. The animals had come to a fork in the tunnel. The moles put their diggers to one path, and then to the other, and then to the first again. They huddled in mole conference, then repeated their examination of the two options.

"Jesus H. Franklin Roosevelt!" said the dog. "The moles are lost."

The bear put his snout to the floor of the tunnel. He sniffed. The cat and dog and moles around him, a yellow whiff of snakeskin, the brown of dirt. And something else, something metallic, rusty.

The bear's nose bumped against . . . a train track.

In the darkness, she could just make it out.

"Here," said the bear. "I found something!"

The dog and cat and moles gathered round.

"Yes, this is the way," said the cat, relieved.

"What is this place?" asked the dog.

"The moles tell me it was a gold mine."

And the moles were right. Not too much farther up the tunnel, the animals came across some old mining equipment. A digger, a jackhammer, great coils of rope. The bear found the place rather spooky and wanted to keep moving, out of the darkness.

They walked, and walked, and walked, until: a glow. Some light seeping down ahead. The animals turned a bend in the tunnel and suddenly had to squint. Ahead, light dappled the tunnel floor. A shaft above, high and narrow. All around them, the detritus of humans. The mine appeared to have been abandoned in haste. Gloves and hard hats were scattered. And, in the center of the shaft, a skeleton.

It was a human skeleton, not a snatch of meat left. Legs at a terrible angle. The sturdy denim work clothes it had once worn were almost entirely disintegrated, just a few scraps and buttons.

"Looks like he fell down the shaft," said the bear, as the animals gathered round.

"Why wouldn't his platoon come and get him?" asked the dog.

None of the animals knew the answer to that. The

bear's throat caught, and she pawed the skeleton. *That's all I am*, she thought. *The seasons come and go; animals are only bone. Just a little more bone than a man.*

The moles, in the half-light, pointed to the side of the tunnel. A hole. It was much smaller, just large enough for the bear to squeeze through.

"That's it," said the cat, "the moles' access tunnel."

The bear wasn't listening. She was lost in her thoughts, staring at the bones.

The dog, though, peered inside. The tunnel slanted up at an angle, into darkness again.

"The human camp," said the cat, "is at the top. Are you ready?"

The dangerous moles bowed.

"Locked and loaded," said the dog.

But the bear hesitated.

"Bear?" said the cat. "Bear?"

Salty tears matted the fur of the bear's snout. She pawed again at the human skull.

She picked it up and looked into its empty sockets.

Chapter 19

Do not ask why the berries are ripe.

This aphorism is usually attributed to a deer, but in our story it is the bear who needed it. For the bear was troubled, there, looking into the sockets of the human skull. Her mind was spinning.

Humanity, or not? I voted for them before. But whether they are worth the struggle, or only chew toys? Better to take my diurnal death, and hibernate, and perhaps dream of honey. What bear thinks she can save a species? This is a human dream, and for all I loved humans, their dreams brought Calamity and death. And what is the dream beyond death? They feared death so. Do I? Ahh, but there's the rub.

*There's nothing in nature that is not in us. We cannot betray
our natures.*

"Bear?" said the cat. "Can you hear me?"

Sinking ever deeper into her own thoughts, the bear
slumped down on the tunnel floor, cradling the skull in
her great paws.

*. . . And I could be out in the sunshine, in a river full of
salmon. Even though the rivers are all green with calamitous waste . . .*

"Bear," barked the dog, "what's the matter? Are you
sick? Do you copy? DO YOU COPY?"

But the bear simply stared into space.

. . . And my cubs were taken from me. I have no grand-cubs for whom I should be risking my fur, pulling myself up into some human camp. They'll probably adopt the cat and dog but skin me and use my fur for hats.

The bear closed her eyes. Her breathing lengthened.

"The bear is . . . shell-shocked, or . . ." The dog was out of breath from barking. "Bear, snap out of it!"

But now the bear was drifting off.

"No, no, bear!" hissed the cat. "Don't go to sleep! Don't hibernate!"

The bear was snoring gently.

"Wake her up, dog! Lick her face!"

"Don't order me around, cat! Why don't *you* lick the sleeping bear's face?"

One of the three moles stood between the dog and cat, holding out its arms as though to make peace. From the folds of its fur, it produced the cocoon timer.

The butterfly was nearly free.

"We have to move," said the cat. "The tunnel won't stay open much longer."

"We can't leave the bear," said the dog.

The moles shook their heads at the bear's behavior.

"Bear, we agreed!" implored the dog. "If we don't stand by the votes, then how shall we ever agree on anything?"

But the bear would not open her eyes.

"Do as you like, dog," said the cat. "I have to keep moving."

And the cat and the moles continued up the tunnel.

The dog stood in the gloom. "Bear," pleaded the dog, "don't leave me on this cat mission alone!"

After a few moments, though, the dog turned and hurried up the tunnel, after the cat.

Chapter 20

At the top of the tunnel, beneath the human camp, the dangerous moles turned to the cat and the dog. The tunnel creaked.

The moles raised their diggers to their snouts for quiet, then dug the last few inches of dirt, up into the human camp.

They peeked over the edge, then dropped back down into the tunnel.

Without any sign to the cat and the dog, they huddled among themselves. One of them pointed, emphatically, in a different direction than the tunnel had been dug. Another batted down his digger, pointed back down the tunnel.

"Well," said the dog, "what's the status?"

"Hmm," the cat purred. "I'll see."

The moles broke their huddle and held out their claws: *not yet.*

The cat ignored them and lightly leapt up for a look.

✦

The perspicacious reader may be wondering, at this juncture, how I, the narrator, could have such intimate knowledge of the events which have been unfolding, and the spectacular events about to unfold, at the top of the dangerous moles' tunnel.

Well you should wonder, and, over the distance which separates us, I applaud your skepticism. It is such skepticism which, like an oxpecker on the hide of the rhinoceros, removes the ticks of untruth. For am I, the narrator, one of the dangerous moles? The cat? The dog? Perhaps the existentially afflicted bear?

Yes, your desire for clarity is admirable. However, I must maintain my anonymity for the moment. No matter how incredible you may find the events which are about to transpire.

✦

The cat peered over the edge of the tunnel.

She was *inside* a hut.

The beams were lashed together with line scavenged from the yacht. The walls were uneven, the roof of pine and sap. The room appeared waterproof but not well insulated. And yet it was . . . homey. Against one wall, two blankets folded upon a steamer trunk.

And beside the trunk, in this otherwise empty hut, sat a little boy, reading a book.

The title of the boy's book has been a matter of debate among not only historians but also laypeople. The crows hold that the book was the first human translation of the history and tenets of Birdism. It has also been reported the boy was reading the human Bible or Koran, even a newspaper from before The Calamity. With humility and due respect for my fellow historians—who have been so eloquently and imaginatively mistaken—I am pleased to put this matter to rest on the basis of sources I will be addressing in section II.

In the meantime, for our porpoises here: when we imagine the boy reading, before he was drawn into this grand misadventure, let us imagine him reading a book which transported him from the lonely hut in which he resided. That conveyed not only the pain of life but some of its joy, some of our pleasures, whether sleeping in the sunshine, hearing the final notes of a blue sheep aria, or knowing, for a little while, the mind of another animal. These are surely blessings, and if, on our way, we may appreciate them a little, perhaps we will be at peace if and when a predator chases us down in old age.

✦

The cat, peeking over the edge of the tunnel, looked at the little boy. Then she darted back down.

"We're inside. And there's no witch," the cat reported.

The moles, accustomed to the vicissitudes of even the best planned missions, were nonchalant.

"I thought your squirrel intel told you this was her home," said the dog.

"She must be out," said the cat. "We have to wait till

she returns." The cat paused. "But there's a boy in the hut. A small boy."

"And what are we going to do about him?"

"We just wait. The witch will come back."

The cat waited beneath the hole, listening. She could hear the turning of the pages in the little boy's book.

The dog impatiently scratched and fidgeted. *Dammit*, he thought, *have I picked up fleas from these moles?*

And the animals waited, listening. But they heard no one coming or going.

After some time the cat peered up again out of the hole and found . . . the same scene.

A little boy, reading.

Now the cat took a longer look. The boy was totally engrossed in the book. He was, thought the cat, in need of a wash. His trousers were tattered, his feet bare and crusted with mud. He wore an old plaid shirt with patches at the elbow. He was achingly slender. The cat climbed back down into the tunnel.

"Well?" asked the dog.

The moles, shaking their heads, already knew the answer.

"She's still not there."

The dog turned an impatient circle in the darkness.

"This mission is off the rails, cat."

"Calm down," said the cat. "It'll be dark soon, and the witch will come back before night."

Twice more the cat checked, and twice more she

found the little boy reading against the wall. He didn't seem to move at all. Now the sun was setting and the light in the little hut was fading, and still the little boy sat, reading. And then it was dark.

The next time the cat checked, the boy had lit a candle. He was still reading.

"Are you sure you have the right hut, cat?" said the dog. "Bigger missions than this have been scuppered by faulty squirrel intelligence."

"The squirrels know what they saw," said the cat. "We wait."

And so they waited.

Chapter 21

When the cat was next about to check the hut, the dog interrupted.

"I'll have a look this time," said the dog. "Stretch my legs."

"Look, dog," said the cat. "We only have this one tunnel—we can't startle the boy with a bunch of barking and fetching. He might warn all the humans before we can speak with the witch—"

"Startle?" demanded the dog. "I was marine recon in the bacon wars. Don't insult me, cat."

"Wait here," said the cat, and leapt up through the tunnel again before the dog could protest.

The dog turned three circles and sat down in a huff.

✦

This time, the boy was asleep beneath one of the blankets. Moonlight fell across his face. From the little tunnel in the floor, the cat could see out of the hut's door that the weather had cleared. It was a fine, cold night. The boy was frowning in his sleep.

Before The Calamity, the cat had liked looking at human faces. They were almost, she thought, as expressive as cat faces. Each one held secrets, a life. The round cheeks of the toddler, the porous nose of the old man. The cat thought she was good at judging character by looking at faces and judged this boy's to be decent. But the cat also knew that faces were unreliable. Better to stick to the plan and find the witch than to take a chance on an honest face.

So, the cat was wondering, curious, *where will she be?* . . .

And on quiet paws, the cat crept past the boy to the doorway and looked beyond into the human camp. Several other huts, of equal simplicity, were scattered around a firepit. No one to be seen, but in the doorways the cat saw the flickering light of lanterns and perhaps cook fires. She felt a wave of nostalgia for her life as a housecat. Though she enjoyed hunting lizards and birds, she had also enjoyed the tinned dinners and catnip.

But that was another life.

There!

She saw across the camp the silhouette of a woman in a tall hat.

A witch's hat.

But she wasn't coming toward the hut—she was walking away.

The cat followed.

What would she be doing, with no fire, creeping around the edge of camp in the middle of the night? *Perhaps she was going to relieve herself*, thought the cat. But her stride seemed tenser than that. Indeed, it looked to the cat as if the woman were . . . *sneaking* somewhere.

The cat followed her to the edge of the clearing in which the camp stood. Here the forest thickened and the cat had to hurry to keep up with the witch's strides. The moonlight came broken through the treetops and the cat heard all around the animals of the forest at night, going about their business, alert to the woman crashing through the . . .

MEYAAHAOW!

A terrible pain shot through one of the cat's back paws, and she was pulled up short. All the breath left her body.

A snare!

Even as the wire tightened, cutting into the pad of her paw, the cat was aware of the witch. She had stopped.

She was coming back.

✦

Down in the tunnel beneath the hut, the dog was worried. The cat had been gone a long time. Just like a cat to go off mission like this!

"Moles, what do you think? You've worked with her before. Is this standard operating procedure for cat missions? Have we got a bit of a loose cannon on our hands?"

The moles sat cross-legged in the tunnel around him, silent.

"What do you think? Get up there, have a look?"

Still the moles said nothing.

Unbelievable, thought the dog, *these goddamn useless moles*. He decided to investigate on his own. Carefully, he inched his way over the edge of the tunnel.

Jaw on the dirt, he paused, listening.

There was the boy—awake. He was reading again by candlelight. Looked as though he had only a few pages of the book left.

The dog liked the boy immediately. He hadn't spent a lot of time with human children, but his memory of the time he had spent with them was pleasant. On R&R, away from the wars, at human celebrations. Children chasing after him, staring at him, frightened of him, and the grown humans reassuring them, teaching the children how to treat a dog: with respect.

Still, the dog's memory, in his advanced age, was not

so sharp. He wasn't sure he remembered how it was for other dogs with human children. He vaguely recalled meeting dogs at the fences of the bases in the bacon wars who reported that human children were cruel, rock-throwing hooligans. Anyway, it was impossible to predict the behavior of this child in particular, and rule one was: adapt to the mission. Still no sign of the witch. Only the boy. And, the dog suddenly noticed:

Ants.

Around the edge of the hole, a column of carpenter ants, steady in their procession. One of them wasn't looking where he was going and mounted the dog's snout.

"Get down!" shouted another ant. And then a chorus of ants: "Get down!"

But it was too late.

The dog's nose twitched. And he tried—with all his military training—he *tried* to repress what was coming. But he . . . he . . . he inhaled mightily, and . . . the ant *whooshed* up his nostril. . . .

"No!" the ants below cried, in the moment before their brother was rocketed back out, a comet among the droplets of dog snot.

"*ACHOO!*" sneezed the dog.

And in the room, the boy closed his book.

"Hi! Dog! Do you want to come in?"

The dog scrambled back down the tunnel as quickly as his paws would carry him.

The moles looked at him with their cold black eyes.

"The boy!" said the dog, tail wagging madly. "The boy . . ."

The lead mole held his diggers out: *yes?*

"The boy spoke! He spoke *grak!*"

The moles frowned, looking at each other.

"It's bloody impossible," said the dog. "But on my honor, on my word as an officer, I heard him speak grak!"

The moles gestured: *and?!*

"He invited me inside."

And?!

"And that's it!"

The moles shook their heads. The dog was obviously mistaken. Too old for the mission. The stress must have pushed him over the edge. The boy wasn't a witch, couldn't speak grak.

The moles indicated that the dog should calm down, maybe even lie down.

"Don't patronize me, moles. I know what I heard—"

"Mammals!"

From the side of the tunnel, a row of ants interrupted.

"The dog is right," said the ants. "He sneezed one of us and the boy invited him inside . . . *in grak*. We heard. And the cat left the hut."

The moles' tiny eyes went wide.

✦

There is a common misconception, a myth really, that ants don't lie. Even creatures as sophisticated as the cat believed this myth. Its origins are hazy but may have to do with the nature of communication in ant colonies. Ants are constantly communicating with each other, and it was widely believed that if even one ant lied to another, the colony would go haywire. Those long lines of leaf carriers would circle in on themselves or splay out into chaos, what have you. Humans were better informed on this topic than many animals.

But I cannot blame my fellow creatures for their ignorance. The work of dispelling myths is Sisyphean, as ants especially know. For what was underneath that boulder Sisyphus rolled for all eternity? Anthills. Crushed on every ascent and then rebuilt. In the ant version of the story, there is no greedy king who brings this predicament on the colony. It is simply the way things are when humans are around. Ants' relationship with mortality is different from humans'—they expect they may die at any moment, that a drop of rain may stun and sweep them into oblivion. To vertebrates, this may sound like a grim state of affairs, but not to the ants. In ant, it is worth noting, there is no first-person singular, only the plural—no "I," only "we."

But I digress. This is not the place for a disquisition on ant linguistics.

Ants lie as frequently as any other creature. But here they told the truth.

✦

The cat, meanwhile, had never been in a trap before. She'd heard of traps, of course. But pre-Calamity, for a city cat such as herself, the closest she'd come to a trap was a mousetrap. The thought of a cat trap, or rabbit trap, or whatever this was, hadn't even occurred to her. In those panicked first moments she recalled the most horrifying traps she had ever heard of. Also:

The zoo.

When she was a kitten, there had been one close to her home with the humans. She had been able to see it from the balcony, had pitied the animals behind bars there, but was never moved to act on their behalf. *Better dead*, she'd thought as a kitten, *than in a zoo*. Once she'd had a conversation with a revolutionary pigeon who had been trying to organize a zoo break. The pigeon never had any success the cat knew of, but now, with wire snaring her own leg, she regretted how she had dismissed him.

This just a fragment of all the thoughts that rushed into her cat brain before they rushed out again, leaving only the maniacal desire to escape.

The cat scratched and bit the wire madly. She looked at her paw, caught and bleeding. She considered chewing it off.

She could hear the witch coming closer.

And then the witch was upon her, looming, her hat shadowing her face in the moonlight. The cat hissed and bared her teeth, tried to scratch, to escape.

In a single deft move, the witch un-snared the cat, lifted her by the scruff, and dumped her inside a sack.

Chapter 22

As the adventures of the dog, cat, bear, and dangerous moles were unfolding—indeed, even in the moment of greatest drama for the cat—the other animals who had attended the council were on their *own* adventures.

Not all were so dramatic. But it does not behoof the historian to focus only on the dramatic or spectacular. And so—while the cat faced the witch, and the moles struggled with the implications of what the dog and ants reported, and the bear slept (in despair)—the *horse* was back among his fellows to report on the vote regarding the fate of humanity.

Opinion was divided in the herd as to the vote's wisdom. Still, the horses agreed they would support the council's decision—though, being herbivores, they would not be eating the humans, only helping to kill them. There was general disappointment at the lack of sugar cubes, but it was pointed out that in some parts of the world, sugarcane must still grow. It was agreed that after this business with the humans, the herd would set out in search of that delicious plant. In the meantime, the great herd began to make its way to the human camp in the forest.

The other animal emissaries were likewise back with their species. A vast murder of crows had convened. Their meeting, as usual, had taken a long time to begin, on account of the numerous prayers to The Egg. The murder filled the sky with shrieks of approval over the vote even as, in the hearts of the younger crows, doubt flowered. This was many years before the Birdist Schism, but some scholars trace its origins to this meeting—even the origins of Bird Atheism.

The baboons' meeting was much simpler. The emissary's news whipped them into a hooting frenzy. Some did not hoot as hard or as loud, but even the most peaceful baboons were too frightened of the rest to stand up and object. And so all began knuckling their way to the camp, to execute the will of the council.

Chapter 23

In the tunnel beneath the hut, the dog frowned at the ants.

"Ants," he growled, "tell me straight: what do you mean, *The cat went outside the hut?* That's not part of the plan."

"We saw her leave the hut to follow the witch."

"Bloody biscuits," shouted the dog. "Why would the cat do that? Moles, did you know about this?"

The dangerous moles shook their heads.

"Shh!" said the ants. "Listen."

In the hut above their heads, footsteps.

"I'll recon," said the dog. But before he could creep

his way back up to the hole, two of the moles blocked
him and shook their heads again.

"What's this then, mutiny?"

The moles put their diggers to their lips for quiet,
and one produced the cocoon. He held it up for the dog
to see. A crack ran along its side; the butterfly was peeking into the great beyond. Time was running out.

While the dog parsed this news, the third mole crept
up and peeked over the edge of the tunnel.

The witch had returned.

She was looming over the boy, who was again asleep.

"Edgar!" said the witch roughly.

The boy was a light sleeper but wasn't up quite fast
enough for the witch. She gave him a kick in the ribs. The
boy didn't let out a cry—he seemed to be used to this
kind of treatment.

"Shift yourself and gather mushrooms. Cat stew
today. I'm off to borrow Agnes's machete. If that greedy
bitch will even give it to me. If she doesn't, we'll use a
sharp rock."

The witch dumped the cat in the sack heavily on the
floor and walked back out of the hut.

✦

See them there: the boy, watchful, back against the wall.
The cat in the sack tied tightly with a string; the hole in
the corner, a dangerous mole peeking over its edge. The
rosy-fingered light of dawn just beginning to flow over

the dirt floor. The silence in the hut broken only by song-birds in domestic argument.

Then the boy spoke.

"Hello, moles."

The cat distrusted her ears—it sounded foreign, and yet familiar.

Grak in a human voice.

The unflappable moles' hearts raced.

"You can come inside, moles. I won't hurt you."

The moles turned and disappeared down the hole.

The boy sighed heavily. The cat heard him step closer to the sack.

"Hello," said the boy, "hello, cat inside the sack. I'm going to let you out, but don't try to bite me, okay?"

In the darkness of the sack, the cat crouched, ready to leap. She could hear the boy untying the string . . . and the sack was open!

The cat bolted, fast as she could on her wounded leg, to the corner of the hut.

"Wait!" said the boy. "Don't go, I won't hurt you."

But the cat was already down the tunnel. She was in such a fluster that she landed on the dog and the two of them slid a ways, a tangle of paws and tails.

Above, the boy peered down into their tunnel.

"Come back!" cried the boy.

Down in the tunnel, the dog and cat separated and shook themselves off.

"Steady on, cat," said the dog. "You're wounded. . . .

Medic!" The dog smelled the blood dripping from the cat's leg.

"I'm fine," said the cat, licking at her wound. "I'm fine. I have to go back up there."

"Are you mad?" said the dog.

"The boy speaks grak!" said the cat. "We have to speak with him!"

"So what if he speaks grak? They want to make you into stew!" said the dog.

"Then why did he let me out?"

"Psy-ops!" said the dog. "This has primate written all over it. A trap for the rest of us, setting you free to lure us all inside."

"Fine," said the cat, "let's vote on whether to go back up. Moles?"

"Blast it," said the dog, "this isn't a voting situation! This is a question of security, and I'm making the call. You're a civilian, cat, and wounded."

"Come or don't, dog, I'm going to talk to the boy."

And she limped back up the tunnel and into the hut. Growling, the dog followed.

Chapter 24

The boy broke into a grin when the animals reappeared at the edge of the tunnel.

"You came back! Come in, come in! Are you hungry?" The boy opened the trunk and pulled out some mushrooms, which he lay on the ground in offering.

The dog and the cat *were* rather hungry, especially the dog. But neither went for the mushrooms.

"When is the witch coming back?" said the cat.

"Don't worry," said the boy, "she won't be back soon. And she's not a real witch. She's just my aunt."

The cat relaxed a little, stepped into the hut. The dog followed.

"But how . . . how do you know how to speak grak?" asked the cat.

"Well," said the boy, picking up the book he'd been reading, then putting it back down, then picking it up again. "I can't . . . I can't tell you."

"Why in the blazes not?!" barked the dog, greatly agitated. To hear with his own silky ears: *grak* spoken by a *human*—which he had always known to be impossible— and then to be *denied* an explanation! It was infurriating.

One may sympathize with the dog. Or hiss him quiet, like the cat did.

"*Shhhh!*"

The cat, licking a paw, turned to the boy. She was frustrated, too. "Well," she said, "I'm sure you have a good reason why . . . ?"

The boy nodded.

"I promised I wouldn't tell," he said. "It's a secret."

"Hmm."

The cat purred in thought. And it is a testament to the wisdom of this cat that she decided not to press the issue. I know firsthand the frustration of generations of historians who have set out to learn the boy's secret. A whole discipline, really, has sprung up around this quest—a quest I will address in section II. But the cat, while curious, knew better. And anyway, she was in purrsuit of a more pressing goal than knowledge: survival.

"Do any of the *other* humans," she asked, "speak grak?"

"My aunt pretends she can talk to animals, but she can't. Hey," said the boy, interrupting himself (as was his wont), "can you stay here for a minute? I have to go to the woods. I'll be right back!"

✦

If you are fortunate enough to have seen depictions of these fabled moments, you may be surprised, even shocked, at my account. The tree carvings are magnificent, of course, stretching as high as the old human cathedrals and depicting in heroic posture the boy, dog, cat, and moles. In the carvings, they stand on top of a mountain, extending hand to paw, and the sky is full of birds, olive branches in their beaks.

As you read here, however, the truth was less . . . formal.

The educated reader will be familiar with the various excellent historians of the body—but not enough attention is ever paid these scholars. We all spend so much time defecating and sleeping, and yet this is so little in our discourse! It seems to this historian that, recognizing that the Boy Who Spoke Grak was also a boy who had to race to the woods after waking up, we might be more inclined to open-mindedness. For reader, don't *you* have to race to the woods, sometimes, as well? And so aren't *you* like this boy?

Certain more cynical members of the department have argued that this argument is naïve. I recall well how vociferous the opposition was during our last seminar.

But I digress.

✦

While the boy was out of the hut, the cat and dog confurred.

"The witch didn't show the boy any respect," said the dog.

The cat licked her injured paw.

"We'll be with him when he warns the humans," reassured the cat. "We can prove he speaks grak somehow. They'll have to listen to him. Look, he's coming back."

The boy returned, carrying a bit of dried meat.

"Squirrel," explained the boy, placing it next to the mushroom on the floor. "Maybe you want that, instead of mushroom?"

The squirrel jerky *was* appetizing. Even if it might be a piece of their intel team. But the dog and cat held back.

The boy sat down. "Do you want to read what's in the book? Or, or, do you want to go to the creek? I know a place where it's deep enough to swim—you probably won't like that," he said to the cat. "But maybe," he continued, to the dog, "*you* like to swim?"

The cat sighed. The boy was lonely. And as the cat got a good look at him, she saw cuts and bruises, skin stretched hungry over his bones. It looked like a hard life for this boy.

"What's your name?" said the cat.

"Edgar," said the boy.

"Well, Edgar, we can't swim."

"I can swim," said the dog. "I was with marine reco—"

"I mean, we don't have *time* to swim," said the cat, cutting off the dog. "We came here because we need your help. We've been watching you."

"What? We haven't—" began the dog, before a mole prodded him into silence.

"None of the other animals want to talk with me," said the boy.

"They're scared," said the cat. "They don't want to end up like that squirrel."

"I never hurt animals," said Edgar. "But I do eat them, sometimes—"

"It's okay," said the cat. "Animals eat animals. Even when we talk with each other."

"It's true," said the dog, "this is the way of the Animal Kingdoms."

The cat nodded. "But not all the animals agree. Some of them are angry at you."

"At me?"

"At all the humans. Because humans caused The Calamity."

Edgar didn't know what to say to that. He'd barely been born when The Calamity started.

"And they're coming, these animals. They want to eat all the people in this camp."

"They can't do that!" said Edgar.

"They will. Unless you help us."

"But what can I do?"

"You can warn the other people, like your aunt. They have to run away. Get on the water, if they can, escape right now if humanity is to survive."

Edgar thought about this.

"But won't some other animals find us, even if we run?"

"That's why you have to separate," concluded the cat. "They might catch some of you. But the rest could survive."

✦

Like many orphans, Edgar was good at reading people. He knew that if he told the grown-ups in the camp what the cat had said, even with the cat and dog at his side, no one would believe him. They'd find a reason not to. And, worse, they'd not like what he was saying, and they would banish him from the camp. And probably cook the cat and the dog.

But Edgar had an idea.

"What if . . ." Edgar asked the cat, "*I* talk to the other animals! The ones who want to eat us? I can tell them that we didn't mean to cause The Calamity. Then they won't want to come and eat us anymore, right? I'll just tell them the truth!"

"They won't listen." The cat shook her head. "It's a nice idea, but the baboons—"

"What, cat, you think these *humans* will listen?" interrupted the dog. "They caught you in a trap and want to turn you into a stew, and you want to parlay with them?"

"What do you propose, dog? If we bring this boy back, he'll be the first human they kill."

"But they'll kill me anyway," said Edgar, "if I can't get the camp to run away, right?"

To this, neither cat nor dog had an answer.

"So I have to try," said Edgar. "I have to talk to the baboons. Hey look at that!"

The animals had been so engrossed in their argument that they hadn't noticed a green and purple butterfly that had flown up out of their tunnel and was fluttering in the hut.

"Time's up, babies," said the butterfly, in her husky drawl.

"We have to go!" said the cat, hurrying to the edge of the tunnel. "That's the timer! The tunnel is going to collapse. Moles!" She called down the tunnel. "Moles—"

With a great *SCHRUMPF* and a cloud of dust, the tunnel collapsed.

And before the animals could make sense of this new problem, they heard a screech.

"Edgar, you ungrateful, disrespectful . . ." came his aunt's voice from beyond the hut, "why aren't you out here gathering mushrooms! I'll thrash you for it!"

The aunt appeared in the doorway, a heavy machete in hand. When her eyes fell upon the dog and cat, she slammed the door shut behind her, dropping the latch.

There was nowhere to hide. The animals were trapped.

Chapter 25

History has not been kind to Edgar's aunt. While it is true that she exhibited much of the ignorance and craving that brought humanity to The Calamity, it must be remembered also that she herself suffered. I am grateful to the enterprising raccoons who acquired the relevant records from the grounded yacht and donated them to our library, further clarifying her pre-village history. She was a member of the yacht's crew—the pastry chef, assigned to single-bunk cabin D-12. It is clear from the manifest that several family members, including her siblings, were also employed on the vessel, and that they, we may presume, were lost in the storm which brought it aground. The responsibility for a small boy must have worn heavily indeed across her bony shoulders. In this light her cruelties are easier to understand. But, as the marabou storks advise: don't let too much understanding lead to too much forgiveness.

✦

"Aunt," said Edgar, "I was just going to get the mushrooms."

"Don't try to distract me, Edgar. Do you think I'm stupid? You never obey me! No one ever obeys me! You let the cat out of the bag! And what is this mangy old dog you've found? I hope you don't think we're keeping pets! We're going to have cat-dog stew!"

And she let out a horrible laugh.

"Mayday!" whispered the dog.

The cat was looking at the latch, and the door, and the little hole at the top of the hut where the smoke got out, trying to devise an escape.

"Aunt," said Edgar, "these animals are special. I don't think we should—"

But before he could finish, his aunt slapped him hard across his face. The *crack!* of it filled the little hut.

Edgar's eyes watered but he didn't cry.

"If your parents could see you disobeying me like this, they'd be ashamed. Now grab that cat so it's not in the way while I deal with the dog," said the witch, raising her machete.

"Wait," cried Edgar, "wait, tell the cat and dog to do something! They'll do it."

"They'll be in my stew is what they'll do," said the witch. "Now out of the way!"

"Just tell them, tell them anything, Aunt, and they'll do it, you'll see. Tell them to . . . jump on the trunk!"

And in grak, Edgar told the cat and dog to jump on the trunk.

The cat, putting her trust in the boy, did so immediately.

The dog, for whom it was a more diffi-cult leap, did so on the second attempt.

"What trickery is this, Edgar?"

"What do you want them to do, do you want them to . . . stand up on their hind legs?"

And Edgar told the cat and dog to do so, and they did. It wasn't a comfortable pose for either of them.

"Or . . . do you want them to bow?"

And Edgar asked the dog and cat to bow, and they did, there on top of the trunk.

"Or sing?"

The dog and cat looked at each other and then sang out together the only song they knew they would know in common. It is one of the few human songs translated into grak, and beloved:

> *Allons, enfants de la Patrie*
> *Le jour de gloire est arrivé.*
> *Contre nous de la tyrannie*
> *L'étendard sanglant est levé.*
> *Entendez-vous dans les campagnes*
> *Mugir ces féroces soldats?*
> *Ils viennent jusque dans vos bras,*
> *Égorger vos fils, vos compagnes.*
> *Aux armes, citoyens! Formez vos bataillons!*
> *Marchons, marchons!*

It was yowling, but yowling with feeling, and even melody.

Edgar's aunt gawped.

She lowered her machete, just a bit.

"I understand them," explained Edgar. "And they—"

"CHARGE!" barked the dog.

And he did.

Chapter 26

The dog went straight for the latch. The cat followed as best she could with her injury. Edgar's aunt swung her machete but missed. The dog, leaping, unhooked the latch and crashed the door open. Together he and the cat zipped through the aunt's legs and escaped.

"You little fool," they heard her yelling, "you let them get away!"

Edgar, though, didn't stay either. He ran past his aunt, out the door and into the sunshine after the cat and the dog.

"Wait!" he cried. "Wait for me!"

The cat and the dog stopped a little ways beyond the

camp as the boy sprinted to catch up with them. His aunt chased behind, sack in one hand, machete in the other.

"You ungrateful, dirty child!" she yelled after Edgar. "Come back here this instant! How dare you disobey me!"

She stopped at the edge of the camp, bent over, panting. She wasn't an old lady, but she wasn't so young anymore, and the pre-Calamity pandemic had scarred her lungs. She'd never be able to catch Edgar and the animals and she knew it.

Edgar watched her wheezing.

"Auntie, these animals want to help us!"

"After everything I've done for you, this is how you treat me! You want to help *them*! Why them and not *me*? Those filthy, filthy animals."

The dog stood beside the boy. Edgar looked down, tears in his eyes.

"She took care of me," he said.

"She's not taking care of you now," said the dog.

"And in fact," added the cat, "we're *not* filthy. We're very clean. Listen—if you want to help your aunt, you've got to come with us."

Edgar nodded, and the three of them turned to walk away.

"Good riddance then! Go! One less mouth to feed! You'll die out in that forest!"

Edgar turned around angrily. "But I'm trying to save you!"

"Oh," said the aunt, her voice a hive of rotten honey.

"You want to save me! And you save me by disobeying me and going off with these *animals*."

"Don't listen to her, son," said the dog, and put his head against Edgar's leg. "Let's go."

"Edgar," she screamed, changing her tone again. "Please don't leave me! Please!"

Edgar took a deep breath and didn't look back.

They heard the aunt's screaming for a long time as they walked off into the forest.

Chapter 27

"Don't like the look of this," said the dog, as he tramped beside Edgar and the cat among the mighty evergreens. Fallen needles were soft underpaw, and the light was clear where it cut through the trees, but it was a long walk to the grounded superyacht. And in the tree-tops: crows.

"They're watching us. They'll tell the baboons that we're with a human. They'll flank us and tear us apart before the boy ever gets to make his case," said the dog, grimly.

The cat said nothing. She wished there was a more discreet way to make it back to the yacht, too. But what

choice did they have? They had to walk, risk being sur-
veilled by crows and attacked by baboons. The cat was
tired and thirsty, and her hind leg ached where the snare
had cut the flesh, but she put one paw ahead of the other.
She didn't let Edgar see how worried she was.

✦

A ways into the forest, Edgar, the dog, and the cat came
upon an ancient, scummy pond. Green water, midday
light. A dark fish darted away as the dog knelt to drink.
The cat noticed hungrily.

A great brown toad, covered in warts, hopped up out
of the mud, startling the dog.

"Greetins," he croaked. "Lovely day, innit?"

"I've had better," said the cat, licking her injured paw.

"Well lemons lemonade frog juice slime, yeah? But
me 'quatic bruvvers, like, they be havin' a message re:
the hairless chimp."

He flicked his tongue at Edgar.

Edgar didn't understand much of the toad's heavily accented grak, but the cat—who had conversed with
and eaten a number of toads in her time—understood
perfectly. The toad, from across the pond, was relaying
a question from some fish. Grak was spoken underwater,
of course, but in different dialects and slangs. Amphibi-
ous creatures like toads often served as interlocutors
between fish and dry land creatures. Likewise seabirds,
snakes—any creature who could inhabit both worlds.

There is a great tradition of literature that draws on these dual identities, these damp consciousnesses, the crustacean colonial novels and so on.

This toad, however, did not strike the cat as much of a thinker.

"I be catlike: can the geezer grock grak?"

"He can," said the cat. "Edgar, say hello to the toad. Tell him you can understand him."

"Hi," said Edgar. "I can understand . . . *some* of what you're saying, Mr. Toad."

"Right then," said the dog. Having drunk his fill, he shook the slobber off his chops. "On mission. Let's get this boy to the council zone."

"Oy! Me fishy message," said the toad. "Message is: wait here. Hold yer horses, in a manner of speakin'."

"All due respect, toad," said the cat, "we have somewhere to be. Why should we wait here? For what?"

"Lookit, these fishes told me and I'm tellin' you: wait. Right there by that tree."

The toad blinked his great round eyes. He flicked his tongue toward a massive willow tree at the pond's edge.

"Why?" said the cat. "Did they say anything else?"

"Oh yeah, summit like . . . old pond, summit summit, splash."

"Sounds like a code," said the cat.

"'S what the fishes say," said the toad. "I done me part."

And he leapt away.

The sound of water.

"Cat, best keep moving," said the dog. "I don't trust that toad."

But the cat had already gone to investigate the willow tree. It was a perfectly ordinary tree with slender branches and cool green leaves, long and serrated. As they moved in the breeze, they made a soft sound. Bark sap shone in knots along the trunk. The cat laid a paw on a low root and took a deep breath. In the pre-Calamity pandemic, she had lived with a human physician. He did not have a family and so was in the habit, whenever he was at home, of speaking to the cat. Often, sitting at the window, he'd told the cat what a shame he thought the zoo was, how they ought not to keep animals locked up. And here at the pond's edge the cat was seized by a powerful memory: how on one of the doctor's days off, he had sat in the window seat of the apartment with her, scratching her behind the ears and looking at that zoo. "Did you know," he'd asked her, "that aspirin is derived from salicylic acid, which is derived from salicin, which is a glucoside produced in willow bark? Willow trees gave us pain medication."

The cat remembered too how the doctor had been home less and less as the pandemic continued, and then one night he didn't return home at all. When there was nothing left to eat in the apartment, the cat had squeezed out a window into a world of fires, flashing lights, and darkness. The Calamity was underway.

It all seemed like such a long time ago. But it wasn't.

"Cat," said Edgar, who had come to stand by the tree. "I have a question—"

But before he could ask it, he and the cat felt a vibration beneath their feet and paws.

Something was coming.

Chapter 28

"**D**o you hear that?" asked the cat.

"Hear what?" said Edgar, for his hearing was less acute.

With the vibration, a scratching. Just beneath their feet.

"There," said Edgar, "look!"

In the shade of the willow, a patch of green grass sank away into a hole. The hole expanded, and dark brown dirt sprayed up into the air.

The three moles somersaulted up out of the tunnel, landing with perfect stillness upon one of the willow's roots.

They bowed.

"Outstanding!" said the dog.

The moles pointed to their new access tunnel.

"Can Edgar fit through there?" asked the cat.

The moles nodded. Edgar looked warily into their dark hole.

✦

The audacity of that boy! Some argue that all history is, at bottom, the history of Great Creatures. The leaders, the creators, these Great Creatures who plunge into unknown mole holes. They set the model and pattern for what the wider masses do—or try to do. Human thinkers in this line argue that everything we see accomplished in this world sprang from the mind of some Great Creature, and so our history must concern itself with their lives in particular. The rat who traveled with Napoleon. The wallaby who taught Elvis how to sing. The lobsters who elevated Salvador Dalí's conceptual practice. The raccoon who, quite disastrously, advised Calvin Coolidge. All the adders socializing with Cleopatra, and of course Mafdet, whom we discussed earlier. Yes, when I think of Edgar leaping down into the unknown, I am filled with pride! And for a moment inclined toward the extraordinary creature theory of history.

But then I remember: Edgar was a child in a camp erected on account of a Calamity caused by millions, billions of other creatures. Every Great Creature lives and dies and marks their territory in a context! A true understanding of history is neither Biography nor Context alone. If I were to rename our discipline: Animal Contextography . . .

But I digress.

✦

The cat was impressed with how easily Edgar shimmied down the tunnel. It was rocky and dark, and he was surrounded by wild animals, but Edgar . . . was happy. He had begun asking a lot of questions: "Where are we going?" "Can all animals speak . . . grak?" "Why don't you moles talk?" "I thought cats and dogs didn't like each other?"

The cat answered as best she could.

A little ways along the dark tunnel, they came upon the train tracks they'd followed in, and resting upon them: a cart. The animals didn't pay it much attention, but Edgar, who had heard of things mechanical from fellow humans, was entranced.

"Wow!" he said. "Does this work? Can I drive it?!"

He got in and pushed the ignition button.

"Jump in!" said Edgar, and the animals climbed aboard the humming cart.

Edgar, experimenting with the controls, pushed the throttle ahead and *SCREEAFWOOSH!*

They zoomed down the tunnel.

"Yahh!" shouted Edgar in joy.

What had taken the animals hours on paw was taking mere minutes in the cart. The dark walls flew past, and tunnel wind ruffled their fur and Edgar's hair.

"Wait," shouted the dog, as they picked up speed. "We can't leave the bear! She's just up ahead."

"A bear?" said Edgar.

"The bear lay down and didn't want to move," explained the cat in the rushing wind.

"I won't abandon the bear!" barked the dog. "No animal left behind!"

And the dog slapped his paw on the kill switch, and the cart stopped.

Ahead in the gloom, the bear lay in the same position in which the animals had left her.

"What's wrong with the bear?" asked Edgar.

The moles shook their heads in shame.

"Doesn't matter," said the dog. "She's one of our own and we're not leaving her."

On his crickled old legs, the dog climbed out of the cart and approached with great care. After all, she was a sleeping bear.

"Dog," called the cat after him. "She doesn't want to come. Leave her be!"

The bear wasn't really hibernating, but she wasn't quite awake either. She was in between, half listening, half lost.

"Bear," said the dog, "bear, wake up!"

The bear didn't stir.

"Bear," said the dog, "the mission! We've got a human who speaks grak. We're bringing him back to the others, to stop the attack."

The bear growled. Ducking down inside the cart to hide, Edgar looked to the cat, whose hair was on end. He was still a little boy, in a dark tunnel, with a bear, and he stroked the cat for comfort, and the cat let him. (Actually, quite enjoyed it.)

"Bear . . ." said the dog.

"WHAT?!" The bear's roar echoed in the cave. "What do you want, dog?"

The dog, a veteran and patriot, stood his ground.

"We leave no creature behind," he said.

The bear's eyes flashed. Coal and light. She bared her teeth.

"We?" said the bear. "Who is we? I am no dog. I am no cat. I am no mute mole. You creatures imagine you may save the humans. But you're the ones who'll need saving."

"I won't leave you behind," barked the dog.

"You are a fool, dog. This cat has brainwashed you. And for what? For *humans*? I was there, dog, at the center of their story machines. Hollywood! They said, 'The bark of history is loud, but it sounds toward justice.' Ha! Now look at them. Even if they had banded together and achieved their dreams, it would have been too late. The Calamity was underway before they could have stopped it. They deserve to be baboon chow."

Silence in the tunnel. But after a moment, the cat spoke up.

"Why then," she asked, "did you vote to save them, bear, if you feel this way?"

"I was in a better mood," said the bear, ice in her voice. "Everything is mood. Perception! You're only chemicals, cat. See what happens when the water in your brain turns black. Leave me here in this tunnel. All is death, in the end."

"Uhh, Mr. Bear," said Edgar, peering up over the edge of the cart. "Hello."

"Psst," whispered the dog. "That's Ms. Bear, lad."

"Hi there, Ms. Bear?"

Now the bear sat up.

"Say that again," said the bear, disbelieving her ears.

"Hello," said Edgar.

"How did you . . . you can speak grak!" said the bear, paw on her heart.

"I don't know," said Edgar. "I just listened, and read. But Ms. Bear, do you really think I should be . . . baboon chow?"

The bear rose. Even on all four paws, her head was higher than the cart. If she wanted to, she could have seized Edgar in her teeth. Edgar gripped the edge of the cart but didn't duck down as the bear put her snout right up to his face. He could smell her bear breath, feel its heat.

"Aren't you afraid, boy?"

"Bear," barked the dog, "what's this, then, bullying this boy?"

"Answer me," said the bear. "For if you are afraid, the baboons will know, and they will tear you apart."

Edgar stayed still and pulled his gaze back from the bear's teeth to her eyes.

"I guess I'm afraid," said Edgar, "but isn't it like you said? 'All is death' anyway? So it's like I told the cat: I have to try."

The bear laughed. "You're just a child," she said. "You don't understand."

"I do understand!" said Edgar. "I understand you're just a sad bear, lying here by herself in the dark."

And the bear knew it was true, and was ashamed.

"But you don't have to be," said Edgar. "You can come with us. Will you?"

◆

The bear's decision would have tremendous consequences. As historians, how are we to understand it?

First, I will say that we cannot understand history without *biology*. Some of my colleagues in certain schools of social science find biology to be irrelevant, even ideologically suspect, in our line of work. They are, sadly, blinkered. By the same token, biology cannot explain *all* history, no matter what the molecular fundamentalist lemurs insist. It remains equally important to take into account "social" or "cultural" behaviors. A balance must be struck. In the final analysis, it makes no sense at all to distinguish between aspects of historical behavior which are "biological" and those which are "cultural."

Which brings us to the bear. How to understand her decision. What will it be?

The boy's vocal cords vibrate, creating sound waves. These are transmitted through the tunnel air to the bear's ears, where in turn the eardrums vibrate. Physics. The bear says yes or the bear says no. If you are a psycho-neuroendocrinologist, you might explain the decision based on the rise or fall of bear testosterone levels in certain parts of the bear's brain, making her more or less aggressive. If you are a bioengineer, you might say that the "yes" or "no" depended on the long muscles around the bear's mandible allowing it to move her jaw into the shape necessary to form words in grak. And if you are an evolutionary biologist, you might say that the bear decided one way or the other because over the course of millions of years, bears that responded in this way to stimulus stood a better chance of passing their genes on to the next generation of bears.

And so on. I, a humble historian (or animal contextographer), would suggest to you that no discipline or explanation, on its own, suffices. Categories have their uses, of course. They help you remember facts. But the boundaries between categories, we would do well to remember, are arbitrary. Once they are set we become too impressed with their importance—like swallows hypnotized by traveling chipmunk magicians and their swinging acorn amulets.

Edgar looked into the bear's black eyes.

✦

The bear took a deep breath.

Shook the cave dust off her pelt.

Then she stood on her hind legs and roared:

"Save the humans!"

"Hoo-raa!" barked the dog. "Onward!"

"But what will you say to the baboons, boy?" said the bear, as she climbed into the cart. "They are not like me."

"I don't know yet," said Edgar, for indeed he did not.

Chapter 29

With the bear on board, the cart was crowded (even with the moles balanced on its edges like surfers). After a few more miles of zooming, the tracks ended in darkness. All clambered out.

Edgar kept close to the dog behind the bear.

"Not to worry," said the dog as they padded along the cave. "There, see, the glow."

Their eyes slowly adjusted from the darkness to the phosphorescence. They had returned to the great underwater salt lake.

"No sign of that lizard," said the dog. "Alright cat,

what's the order of operations here? How do we get back up top?"

The cat had anticipated this problem. To enter, she had carefully climbed down from the mole access tunnel at the top of the cavern. In contrast, the bear and dog, as we saw, slid down the tunnel, flew into the air, and thence down into the salty, freezing lake. The sight had provided the cat some pleasure. Now, however, the bear and dog and boy had no way of getting back up to the mouth of the cave. The wall was too steep. How would they get up there? The cat had hoped there might be a way. Having failed to invent one, she was at this point scanning the cavern for alternative exits.

Edgar and the dog saw the concern on the cat's whiskered face and looked to the bear, who pointed up to the mouth of the mole tunnel high in the cavern wall. "That's how we got in."

"So we're stuck here?" barked the dog. "Classic feline planni—Edgar watch out! There's a scorpion on your leg!"

✦

Here is no place for a discussion of arachnid aesthetics. But one *could* write a whole chapter on the glistening, hairy, eight-leggedness; the markings along the carapace; the webs and eggs.

Some like that sort of thing. I personally am of the opinion that the Australian tarantula self-portraits are among the Animal Kingdom's great artistic treasures. And this scorpion was especially handsome.

But it did look as though it was about to sting and kill this little boy.

✦

Edgar hadn't noticed the scorpion. Then he did and was frightened. But instead of batting it away or freezing, Edgar tried to look it in the eyes and talk to it. His voice shook as he did.

"Hello, scorpion."

"Careful, Edgar!" hissed the cat.

The dog growled. He had known a ridgeback who had died of a scorpion sting in the bacon wars—and a grown human soldier who, not shaking out his boots one morning, had been stung into a coma.

"Shh!" Edgar told the dog. "He's saying something."

"You're standing on my nest."

The scorpion's voice was very quiet. Edgar bent down close to its pincers to hear.

"You're standing on my nest," repeated the scorpion.

Edgar raised a foot and, to his dismay, found that he was standing on a small hole in the dirt.

"I'm sorry!" he said, stepping away. The scorpion hopped off his leg, pincers clicking.

"What . . . animal are you?" said the scorpion. "I have never heard your voice before."

"I'm a human boy," said Edgar. "Can't you see me?"

"We cave scorpions don't have eyes. But I can feel your vibrations. And I can hear you. We have heard, down here, that many animals have decided to kill you . . . humans."

"Get away from that scorpion, Edgar," growled the dog.

The scorpion raised his stinger higher and mock charged the dog.

The cat crouched to pounce.

"Wait!" cried Edgar, jumping between the cat and the scorpion. "What do you think of that?" he asked the scorpion. "Should the animals kill us humans?"

"No abovegrounder has ever asked my opinion before," said the scorpion.

All were silent, waiting for the scorpion to continue. It clicked its pincers in thought.

"And now, without warning, a human asks me. What do I think? I think vertebrates and mammals and all the above-grounders will never be fair. And I know they are no better than insects; we're all the same. Bears seek out caves, do they not? The hard walls of the cave are not so different from the hard plates of my back. And yet in the animal councils you have drunken monkeys and idiot horses, lions who can't count higher than their claws, superstitious birds, ignorant of life on the ground. *These* animals may join animal councils, while we insects and arachnids can't? None of us? Oh, you say, insects *choose* never to come. No! We choose to *survive*. The *structures* prevent us from joining their councils and participating. We cannot come into the light to join the council. We'd get eaten immediately! And yet the council is held on a cliff top, in the afternoon."

"That doesn't sound fair," said Edgar.

"But what is to be done?" asked the cat, who had, in her time, killed and eaten a scorpion. "The world is too large and various to include every creature in every council."

"Same as always," said the scorpion. "Such careless cat contempt has driven the cockroaches into mindless, collectivist violence."

"Scorpion, you should come with us!" said Edgar. "All the cave insects should come if they want. We wouldn't let any of the other animals eat you. We'd be your eyes. Right?"

The other animals, with their deep distrust of stinging bugs, were silent. But Edgar insisted.

"Right?!" he said.

Reluctantly, all the animals nodded their heads, muttering their assent.

"In that case, I would love to come to the council," said the scorpion.

And in a blink, he climbed onto Edgar's shoulder.

The cat and dog stiffened. At any moment, the scorpion, if he so chose, could plunge his stinger into the boy's neck. Edgar stiffened too but then tried to relax. He remembered being swatted by his aunt and resolved not to swat the scorpion. Which would probably kill him if he did anyway.

"Okay," said Edgar. "The problem is, we all need to get up to that tunnel."

"Hmm," said the scorpion. "Maybe I have some friends who can help."

◆

This is a work of history and animal contextography rather than pure mathematics, but as we have established, the disciplines are inextricable. What happened next requires some numbers. The average cave ant can support five thousand times its body weight. The average adult female grizzly bear weighs between three hundred and four hundred pounds. This bear, as we have noted, was not a particularly well-fed bear. Dividing pounds by ants, we find that a minimum of thirty thousand ants are necessary to lift a bear. And this is a minimum—a minimum!—of nine 4,000-ant-strong colonies.

Again, I am no mathematician. But this is, roughly, how many ants would have been required.

But how about . . . flying cave bugs? How many post-Calamity mutated *Troglocladius hajdi* were there?

A lot, is the answer, and a lot of other cave bugs, too. Pre-Calamity, *T. hajdi* had been the only flighted underground insect—but post-mutation, the flight had spread rapidly in the world's darkest places. And that day, such an array of flying cave insects as you have never imagined heeded the scorpion's call. Ants and skull beetles and floating worms, winged-pseudoscorpions and millipedes and centipedes. A buzzing, clicking tide. All swarming around Edgar's feet, and then gently taking hold of him . . .

"Steady on, steady on," yelped the dog, as he felt the bugs' embrace.

"Thanks no," said the cat to the bugs. "I'll make my own way." And she leapt, climbing up the steep wall to the access tunnel's mouth. There she turned to watch an unprecedented takeoff.

Insect latched to insect latched to insect. The whole swarm's power pulsing, tiny leg to tarsal pad to claw . . . One or a thousand or a million would never have moved the bear an inch.

But in the vast cavern, *billions* of insects linked up.
BUZZZZZZZ . . .

The swarm gently encircled the animals and slowly, steadily . . .
BUZZZZZZZ . . .

"*Wheels up!*" cried the dog. "*Dog aloft!*"

"Yahoo!" cried Edgar, flying up over the lake.
BUZZZZZZZ!

And the bear was airborne. As she rose, the despair she'd known . . . floated away. Her mind cleared. Soon she'd be back in the sunlight. The sunlight that made berries, and honey, and the glint off a salmon's scales.

Gently, the swarm deposited her great bulk beside the cat, at a slanted tunnel's edge, high in the cavern wall. The bear looked out over the great underground lake and down at the shore where she'd come from. For a moment, at least, she'd been a *flying* bear. And as she turned around into the darkness of the tunnel she felt, for the first time in her life, love for insects.

Edgar and the dog and the moles were already there, waiting in the gloom.

The moles bowed to the swarm.

"Collective action," said the scorpion. "Onward!"

And the swarm buzzed to Edgar:

"*GOOD LUCK.*"

Chapter 30

As the animals trooped up the steep tunnel, the cat laid out a plan.

"As you know, no animal invited to the council-place can be harmed by another animal. Edgar is now invited by us, but the law doesn't hold until he gets there. So, when we get out of the cave, we'll form a circle around him, to hide him until we get to the safe zone."

"Good copy," huffed the dog. It had been so much easier falling *down* this tunnel.

"Bear, you'll take the lead. If Edgar can't convince the baboons and the rest to let humanity live, we're going to have to fight our way out. I'm not going to lie to you:

this could be a suicide mission. But it is humanity's only chance."

The animals climbed uphill for a little while in silence. The cat wished she had a better plan than one boy who spoke grak. Would Edgar's *words* convince the baboons and all the other animals? Probably not. But what else did they have? She looked at Edgar, wide-eyed in the gloom, between the old dog and the ragged bear, tiny scorpion on his shoulder.

✦

Finally, Edgar and the animals reached the cave where their adventure had begun. It was still dry, the pile of bones was still in the corner, the glow of the post-Calamity Spanish moss still lit the walls. But in one important respect, it was different.

It was occupied by a baboon.

Not the baboon who had been a member of the voting council—a *different* baboon.

A baboon with long, curling, white eyebrows.

"So," said this baboon, "it's true. . . ."

The cat froze, the dog growled, the bear tensed.

"I'd heard rumors, but I didn't believe . . . a cat, traveling in the company of a human who . . ."

The baboon galumphed over to Edgar and gave him a sniff.

"Is it true? Does he speak . . . ?"

"Hello, Mr. Baboon," said Edgar.

"He does!"

The baboon slapped the ground in hooting excitement.

"So, you've caught us," said the cat, "but before you tell the other baboons—"

"Caught you?" said the baboon. "Cat, you've got it wrong. I haven't caught you. I want to *join* you. To *help* you."

"I smell a double agent," growled the dog. "Cover his flanks, bear."

"When they heard from the crows that you were with a human, many of the baboons went in search of you. They wanted to tear your arms off. It is wise you took an underground route back. But many baboons are not *all* the baboons. Baboons are not a monolith. Species does not determine what an animal thinks. You see, I am with . . . *the baboon opposition*."

"What's the baboon opposition?" asked Edgar, thoroughly confused.

"There is always an opposition. Even within oppositions. Even within a single baboon. Some of us did not want to send anyone to the animal council at all! We saw no need. The whole idea—kill all humans—was ridiculous. Why would we participate? Especially without the participation of our insect and arachnid brothers?"

The scorpion dipped its tail in acknowledgment.

"Now," said the baboon, "the baboon opposition has made inroads with the majority, and they are willing to reconsider the vote. And since it's true you have a human who speaks grak, I think they'll reconsider! I think we can win."

"How can we trust this baboon?" growled the dog.

"Dog, you do me wrong," said the baboon.

"We have no choice," said the cat.

"We do!" growled the dog. "The bear and I can make a chew toy out of this lying ape."

The cat held up a paw. "We came to change minds. This baboon offers his support. We can't turn away from new friends because of old grievances."

"But—"

"Dog, listen. It is as he says. Not all baboons are of a single mind, any more than all dogs are."

The dog reluctantly quieted his growl.

"Thank you, cat," said the baboon, smiling, "for your trust. Shall we go? We must speak with the rest of the animals as soon as we can, before they set off for the human camp."

The cat looked from the bear to the moles to the scorpion to Edgar to the dog, who reluctantly saluted.

"Let's go."

Outside the cave, the dusk.

The animals wound up the cliff side in single file.

Reaching the top, some ways from the end of the promontory, they beheld an incredible sight.

Chapter 31

The cliff where the animals had voted was *packed* with baboons.

The smell was phenomenal.

A thousand baboons, perhaps more. Ten thousand!

Learned readers may say, "Impossible!"

But, I assure you, at least a thousand baboons. This stretch of seaside woodland was thick with them, a great whooping, hacking, arguing, feces-throwing, fur-rending maelstrom, much engaged in lovemaking and arguing and pounding of the earth as they waited for . . . the signal.

And in the trees above them, crows. These outnumbered the baboons three to one, perhaps more. It was an unholy racket they were making. *Caw caw caw!* A whole battalion singing their tremendous hymns, which had driven off the other birds for miles. And not just the other birds. Though the crows and the baboons had, per the agreement at the council, spread the word about the decision to eat all the humans, no other species had massed with them. The original baboon emissary, whom we came to know earlier, was frustrated by this, but finally he decided it did not matter. He was certain the baboons would finish off the remaining humans. They didn't need any other species' help! And he, personally, would be certain to approach the battle from the rear. Plenty of idiot baboons to go ahead of him. He started a chant, to rile them up:

"Eat the children! Eat the children!"

Other baboons joined in.

"Eat the children! Eat the children!"

Shocking?

But why should it be?

Why, indeed, this historian would ask, are we continually surprised by the rapacity, violence, and arrogance of those creatures who ascend to leadership? Do we not recall, throughout animal history, the despots and fools who have so handily outnumbered the saints? History is a dark tale that doesn't wag. Which is not to endorse that sad bear. Oh no! Only to remind you, reader: look to history before you cast your vote. And to you readers who are unsurprised, who have looked to the history, I say: Bravo! Do not falter in your work. The barbarians may tell you writing is a waste in these post-Calamity times, mere entertainment, the frivolous misdirection of resources, a lost cause. Ignore such animals. History is as vital as water.

But I digress.

"Eat the children!"

Now the horses arrived. Not so many as the baboons, but several hundred at least, a great herd, trotting and then slowing in the simian crowd. The grass on the promontory was thinning rapidly. Hundreds of tails whisked away clouds of flies. The flies were uninterested in joining the attack on the humans, they informed the horses, but would come along when it was finished and lay eggs in the bodies.

"Eat the children!"

✦

Edgar and our band of creatures watched the crazed baboons chanting from a ways off. The dog remembered well the mood of incipient mayhem from his days at war.

"Maybe," said the cat, "we should revise the plan."

"Many of them are baboon opposition," said the curly eyebrowed baboon. "You will be safe among them. Keep a circle around the boy until he is at the council safe zone, and all will be well."

"The baboons tried to rip you apart, cat, don't you remember?" interjected the dog. "What's to stop them from ripping us all apart if we walk up there? This is a bad plan!"

The cat looked at the curly eyebrowed baboon, taking his measure again.

They'd come this far.

"Keep your nerve, dog," said the cat. "It's not us they're after. It's humanity."

"Edgar is human!" cried the dog.

"And when they hear him speak their language," said the cat, "they'll listen. You said so yourself. If we can only get him to the council safe zone, by that yacht."

"I'm not afraid," said Edgar.

"Then neither are we," said the cat.

The bear put a heavy paw on Edgar's shoulder.

"I'll go first," she said.

The animals formed a circle around the boy and walked into the sea of baboons.

✦

At first, the baboons didn't notice. They were expecting, per the agreement at the council, contingents of bears and cats and dogs to join them in the attack on the camp, and the moles exploded smoke bombs to further confuse them.

Edgar stayed very close to the bear as baboons gnashed and growled all around him. The bear swatted the baboons away, clearing a path to the smashed helicopter where the council rules held.

Finally, they arrived and broke the circle. As the moles' smoke cleared, the first baboons caught sight of Edgar and howled.

News rippled across the cliff side, and the noise redoubled.

"Baboons!" cried the cat, leaping up to her old seat in the cockpit of the smashed helicopter. "Listen! This boy can speak grak! He's come to speak for the humans!"

But the cat could not be heard over the din of furious primates. They were hooting, leering, teeming across the cliff.

One jumped at Edgar, but the bear smacked him down.

The crowd shrank back, then surged.

The horses had seen the commotion and were trotting over. Crows were flying in as well. They had left the trees and were settling thick upon the yacht overhead, cawing and screeching.

"Listen," shouted the cat again, to no avail. "Bear, dog, help me!"

The dog barked, loud as he could, that the boy could speak grak.

"Listen to him," barked the dog.

"Listen!" roared the bear.

"No, YOU listen," screamed a baboon back at them. "Eat the children!"

"Kill the human lovers!" shouted another baboon.

"Eat the children!"

"Praise to The Egg!" shrieked a vast murder of crows.

"Wait!" cried the cat. "Council zone rules! We voted, we were civil with one another, we can be again! Where is the baboon opposition?!"

The cat searched desperately for the curly eyebrowed baboon.

For a moment, she couldn't find him—then she spotted him in the crowd.

He was standing among a contingent of mice.

Mice who, at that very moment, were passing him . . . a shining bell.

The curly eyebrowed baboon took it and regarded his reflection happily. He rang the bell and hooted, arms in the air.

"Down with cats!" he shouted.

The mice raised their tails and locked eyes with the cat.

"Eat the children!" chanted the baboons.

And Edgar was frozen with fear.

As the baboons closed in around Edgar and his friends, the dog howled. Several of the baboons had him by the tail.

"Wait!" cried the cat, as baboons rocked the smashed helicopter. "Wait, just talk . . ."

The moles were now engaged in fierce paw-to-paw combat. A pile of baboons grew around them. But the moles knew they were outnumbered. They prepared themselves for death.

The bear kept batting away baboons as they lunged at Edgar, but she was tiring. Soon she would fall.

The sky was darkening with crows.

But then: a roar.

At the base of the promontory, the giant cave lizard.

"SQUEAK ON!" roared the lizard.

He was charging toward them, flapping his arms like they were bat wings. And riding on his scaly back, a creature Edgar had never seen before: the goda.

The dog caught sight of the goda too, between the mass of baboons, and his heart leapt.

"Goda!" he barked, tail wagging madly. "Watch out, my darling!"

But before the giant lizard and goda could reach him, the horses stampeded. The baboons had driven them into a frenzy. The herd charged the lizard. It went down in a crush of hoofs, and the baboons were upon him next. The goda fell, and the dog lost sight of her.

"Aaaaooooooo!" howled the dog, as a baboon bit him to the bone.

He felt the blood begin to seep away. . . .

With the last of her strength, the bear lifted Edgar upon her shoulders.

"Speak, boy!" pleaded the bear, "if only to these nearest creatures."

But Edgar was too frightened. He couldn't make his mouth work. Everything inside was shaking and cold. The cat leapt upon the bear beside him.

"What do I say?" said Edgar, in a voice so small no one could hear him except the cat and the scorpion on his shoulder.

"The truth!" said the scorpion.

"Fine, truth," said the cat, "but also you must give them something! Make them a promise!"

"But what?"

As the baboons closed in, the cat remembered life before The Calamity.

She remembered what humans were really like.

And she gave Edgar an idea. She knew what to promise.

She wasn't a kitten anymore.

✦

At first, it was only the baboons closest to Edgar who stopped howling. Once they stopped, more could hear him shouting from his perch on the bear. Some were so surprised to hear a human declaiming in grak that they instantly froze. Others took longer, but then they crowded in, shushing each other. Those closest sat down around the bear's paws, looking up at the boy, and others sat behind, until soon many dozens were sitting in silence. Edgar yelled to reach those at the edge of the seated circle. The horses quieted too, leaving the giant cave lizard and goda bloodied but alive.

All around, baboons and crows on the backs of the horses strained to hear the little boy.

And Edgar shouted, as the cat had advised:

"I speak your language!" he cried. "And I promise, I *promise . . ."*

Postscript

Just after sunset on March 19, in this Post-Calamity Year 81, I climbed into the Professor's treehouse. Professor Edgar was seated at his desk. It was, as usual, strewn with bark paper and books, quills and pots of the various liquids he used for ink. At first I thought he was asleep, peaceful as he seemed, chin on his chest, eyes closed. As though he had simply paused in his studies for a nap. Alas, our beloved Professor had passed away.

Amidst the clutter on his desk, I discovered this unfinished manuscript. It was with love for my old friend, humility, and some trepidation that I took on the task of editing what the Professor had begun and offering this modest context.

As the oldest human in The Zoo—to our knowledge, the oldest human on earth—Professor Edgar enjoyed great respect not only from his fellow humans, but from the many animals who visited, viewed him and his species through the fence, and studied with us. I know firstpaw their respect was not simply for his age and erudition, but for his generosity. Though he could certainly be verbose—and became more so in old age—his mind was clear at the end as it had been throughout his long life. It was the Professor, more than any other creature, who turned The Zoo into the center of learning it is today.

Those of us born after the establishment of The Zoo often asked the Professor to tell the story of how it came to be. The cat, dog, bear, moles, and other creatures directly involved have all since passed away, and their species' accounts—recorded in The Zoo archives, passed down through the generations—are conflicting. The Professor promised he would put it all down on bark—or at least tell us the story so we could remember it—before his demise. We can be grateful for the start of it he made here, even as we mourn all that he left unwritten.

Professor Edgar often said that humans were the animal least suited to life on this planet. What other creatures arrive to life so helpless, and without claws or wings or other useful adaptation? And what creature does more mischief? Humans' only saving grace, he said, is that they are good scholars. And what makes a good scholar? The question was the subtext of our whole life together, but I only recall asking him directly once. Professor Edgar had furrowed his brow.

"Imagination," he had replied, "and working well with baboons."

Which brings us to the final pages of the Professor's unfinished account. Impressed though the gathered baboons, horses, and crows were, they were not ready to grant mercy to humanity solely on the Professor's fateful promise: that humans would confine themselves to The Zoo. For their own safety as much as all of ours, the humans were required to build a fence around their camp. They did so rapidly, under threat of death.

Thereafter, life inside consisted, mostly, of what the Professor liked to do—read, listen to stories, recite them aloud, and write them on tree bark. As he grew up, Professor Edgar systematized the written and oral traditions of The Zoo in which I write now. The early days were difficult. Most animals, back then, came only to throw feces at the humans and ogle them. But as years passed, many more came to speak with Professor Edgar and the other humans who, under his tutelage—and the threat of violence from baboons at Zoo's edge—finally learned to speak grak. Even the Professor's aunt.

Professor Edgar's account provides invaluable context for this history. Still, when I finished reading, in the moonlight of that early spring night, I was consumed with curiosity. The Professor had promised humans would live in a zoo, but was that promise really enough? What *exactly* did the Professor say that day, so long ago, when he stood on the bear's back? One promise hardly seems enough to have convinced a mob of angry baboons. But then, what *could* a child have said to account for humanity, given The Calamity? To prove its goodness? To prove, in the face of so much evidence to the contrary, that humans are decent animals?

Sadly, direct knowledge of the speech has also passed away with the Professor. We are left to piece it together from other sources—not a simple task. The Professor's account suggests the baboons began to sit down and listen when they heard him speaking grak, but several near-contemporary accounts dispute this characterization. In the Birdist histories, Professor Edgar is seen flying over the baboons (with the help of a supernatural feather), and he convinces all present in that miraculous manner. Several insect accounts draw our attention to the *rules* of The Zoo as evidence that the Professor and the baboons were engaged in classic mammal realpolitik. The moles, as usual, are silent on the matter.

The issue is more than academic. I am certain those of us who remain sympathetic to humans could make use of the Professor's long-lost arguments, as debates on humanity continue. One rages even today—regarding several humans' recent attempt to escape The Zoo. Apprehended by alert baboons, the accused have pled for their lives, and we are in council again to decide their fate. The would-be escapees insist that their *fellow* humans, by hoarding the available nuts and berries, forced a choice between flight and starvation. I suspect this defense will wither under guinea fowl cross-examination and the accused will be fed to a pack of wolves. In the Professor's spirit, however, several foxes and I will be arguing for understanding, for mercy, and even—trying though it may be—for *loving* the humans.

What else, after all, can we do?

> Top Goda-Dog in Charge of the Library
> Post-Calamity Year 82
> The Zoo

Acknowledgments

At Henry Holt and Company, I've had the good fortune to work with Natalia Ruiz, Janel Brown, Helen Carr, Chris Sergio, and the inimitable Sarah Crichton; thank you all. Thanks also to my agents, Eric Simonoff and Bob Bookman, for their ongoing counsel and many years of friendship. Thanks to Rozina Ali and Musab Younis and for their notes, especially on bacon and scholarship of the body. And thank you, Thomas McDonell and Alice Whitwham, for close reads, animal wisdom, and much else besides.

About the Author

Nick McDonell is the author of the novels *Twelve, The Third Brother,* and *An Expensive Education,* as well as a book of political theory, *The Civilization of Perpetual Movement,* and five books of reportage, *Guerre à Harvard, The End of Major Combat Operations, Green on Blue, The Widow's Network,* and *The Bodies in Person.*